NO DIRECTION HOME

HOME

THE REVENANT

BOOK 4

MIKE SHERIDAN

Editing by Felicia Sullivan

Proofreading by Laurel Kriegler

Cover art by Deranged Doctor Design

CHAPTER 1

The executions were a grim affair. At 2 p.m., three of Mason's eleven surviving gang members were selected by a team led by Bert Olvan and taken out of Sequoya, one of Camp Benton's family cabins, where they were being kept under heavy armed guard.

Outside, the men were cuffed and escorted down a forest path that led to the north end of the headland. All three had wary expressions on their faces. They sensed that the direction they were being taken in didn't bode well for their future.

"Where you taking us?" one of them finally piped up, a skinny man in his forties with lank, dark hair, and a hangdog look not helped by his current circumstances.

"You're off to meet Mason," Bert Olvan replied gruffly, walking alongside him, his pistol held loosely by his side.

The man's step faltered. "B-But we heard Mason is dead!"

It had been several hours since the combined Benton and Eastwood forces had retaken the old YMCA camp and the remains of Mason's crew rounded up. News of their boss's demise had quickly reached the surviving prisoners via their guards.

"You heard right. But you're going to meet him all the same." Olvan prodded the man in the back. "Now move it. We don't have all day."

Five minutes later, the group emerged from the forest and stepped out onto North Beach's stony shoreline. At the far end of the bay, set ten yards apart, three wooden posts stood at the spot where Russ had been executed several days ago.

Spotting them, all three prisoners came to a halt. "Please mister…" one of them, a big, broad-chested man wearing a short-sleeved camo shirt, whispered hoarsely. "Just let us go. We'll leave the area for good. That's a promise."

"The only place you're going to is the bottom of a ditch," Olvan growled. He stared at the man fiercely. "See, I was there that night you captured Ray Faber. I saw you haul him over to the bonfire where Mason executed him like a dog. I saw you laugh your head off at the sight. That's why I picked you out first today—to honor my friend. Ray was a good man. He didn't deserve to die like that."

The remaining color drained from the bandit's face. Knowing any further discussion was futile, he trudged up the beach alongside his two companions, head bowed.

When they reached the posts, the three were separated. Starting at the ankles, each man's legs and torsos were tightly bound to the posts. Finally, cord was looped around their necks to keep their heads upright.

Once all three were ready, Olvan gave the waiting Sheriff Rollins and the nine-man firing squad the signal. Despite what he'd said earlier that day, when he'd protested against the executions, one of the squad members was Henry Perter. When it came down to showing solidarity with the rest of his companions, he had no intentions of shirking his duties.

Rollins kept things brief. He read out the charges, then asked if any of the prisoners had anything to say. When none replied, the guards shoved a pillowcase over each of their heads. Grouped in threes, each of the firing squad knelt down on one knee, took aim, and fired, sending the three men to meet whatever hell their Maker had in mind for them.

For the next hour, things continued in the same fashion. Having heard the gunshots, the remaining prisoners knew what to expect. Most remained silent as they were escorted through the forest. Some, though, broke down and begged for mercy. None was given, and they had to be dragged to the posts sobbing and screaming.

Finally, the last two men, both too injured to walk, were carried down to the beach on stretchers. Rather than being executed standing, they were sat down at the base of their posts. It was a pitiful sight. One was so badly injured he barely comprehended what was happening. A pillowcase was hastily put over his head, and he and the other man were quickly dispatched.

Their bodies were rolled up in bed sheets and tied at each end, then they were carried on the stretchers back through the forest and up to the parking lot, where Olvan's Pajero sat waiting. Nine bodies were already stretched out in the load bed, their bloodstains seeping through the sheets and onto the metal floor.

Two Benton men jumped into the truck alongside Olvan, who wordlessly started the engine and drove out of the camp. He headed north along Card Spur Road, then, after a few miles, turned up a narrow track and into thick forest. The track petered out and Olvan came to a stop. The bodies were dragged out of the truck bed and unceremoniously dumped in a large hollow to one side of the track.

"The creatures of the forest will eat well today," Olvan said grimly as he climbed behind the wheel of the Pajero again. "Coyotes and wolves don't give a damn about what sort of men these were. They'll eat their hearts and all."

***

At 4 p.m., the joint Benton and Eastwood war committee convened in Camp Benton's council room, where a large flask of coffee and a plate of cookies awaited them. It had only been an hour since the executions, and the mood in the room was somber.

"Nothing pretty about what went down," Ned Granger said, pouring himself a cup from the flask before passing it to Henry Perter sitting next to him. "We just did what we had to do."

Henry Perter grimaced, still ashen-faced from the day's events. "Downright ugly is what it was. I pray to God we never need do something like that again."

Granger patted his friend on the shoulder. "War is an ugly thing, Hank. Even in victory."

For the next while, the group discussed practical matters, such as how the two groups would communicate going forward. The experience with Mason had taught them how vital it was to be in immediate contact. As the distance between the two camps was too great for their handheld walkie-talkies to operate, they needed to come up with another method. Granger suggested that the groups scavenge CB shortwave radios systems that could be installed at both camps. The larger equipment was more suitable for long-distance communications.

Walter agreed, and proposed they use propane generators to power the radios.

"Gasoline quality will start to degrade soon," he told the group. "In a few months, it's going to do nothing but clog up our engines." Across the table, Perter stared at him dubiously. Walter smiled. "I know what you're thinking. This stuff's been in the ground for millions of years, right? Problem is, once it goes topside and gets refined, it's got a short shelf life."

"So how much longer do I get to drive my Harley?" Ralph asked, looking perturbed. He obviously had no idea of this either.

"Hard to say," Walter replied. "Anywhere from a couple of months to a year. It depends on storage conditions, plus a host of other factors."

"Such as?"

Walter shrugged. "Ethanol blends, for example, have shorter shelf lives. Also, it's impossible to know how long it's already been sitting there at the station. We need to get used to the fact that, at some stage, we're going to need to come up with alternate power sources."

"Such as your micro hydro system," Granger said.

Walter nodded. "Soon as I get back to Eastwood, I intend starting on it. Once I've put a system in place and tested it, I'll bring a team over and we'll build yours. A promise is a promise."

"Thank you, Walter," Rollins said. "We appreciate that."

It had been a long, dramatic day, and a short time later they wrapped up the proceedings. Besides, the Eastwoods needed to get back to their own camp soon. Only a skeleton crew had been left behind during the battle with Mason, and Walter was keen to return.

Rollins closed the meeting by saying, "I know I speak for all the Benton council when I say how truly we appreciate your help over these past few days. Not only did you harbor us when we were forced out of our camp, but you risked your lives helping us take it back. Without you, we would never have succeeded in defeating Mason."

"We lost some good people along the way," Granger added somberly. "Let's hope we can put that behind us now and get on with developing our communities."

Mary Sadowski nodded emphatically. "I'll second that." She glanced at Cody briefly before her eyes rested on Walter. "I was wrong about you and your group. I apologize for what I said the other day. You're good people through and through, and I'm proud to have fought alongside you."

Walter smiled deprecatingly. "Thank you, Mary. The feeling is mutual. Over the past few days, our two camps have developed a sense of camaraderie and respect. Long may it last."

On that note, the four Eastwood members rose from their seats, as did the Bentons. After shaking hands all round, Rollins said to Walter, "Would you mind staying behind for a few minutes? There's something I need to run by you."

"Sure," Walter said, slightly surprised. To his companions, he said, "See you in a few."

Cody, Ralph, and Clete filed out of the room, along with the four other members of the Benton council.

"What's on your mind, John?" Walter asked as soon as everyone had left the room, shutting the door behind them.

Rollins drew in his breath. "I have a proposal for you. One you might think somewhat strange considering everything we've gone through these past few days."

Walter stared at him, his curiosity growing. He sat down at the table again and leaned back in his chair. "All right, Sheriff. Hit me with it."

***

"What was all that about?" Cody asked fifteen minutes later when Walter showed up at the parking lot. He and Emma were sitting on the tailgate of Walter's Tundra. Next to them, Ralph and Clete leaned against the side of Ralph's F-150 pickup, both smoking cigarettes.

"Oh, nothing in particular," Walter said casually. "The sheriff just wanted to impress on me how keen he is in setting up good communications between our camps. You can't really blame him after all that went down with Mason."

"Really? That's all?"

Walter nodded. "Yep, that was it." From the look in his eye, Walter knew that Cody didn't quite believe him. He opened the door to the Tundra and climbed in behind the wheel.

Cody slid off the tailgate and walked around the far side of the truck. He opened the front passenger door, and he and Emma clambered inside.

Next to them, Ralph and Clete had gotten into the Ford. Ralph leaned his head out the truck window and stared over at Walter. "That answer don't wash with us for one second, Walter." He started his engine. "So, guess who don't get invited to the party tonight? It's gonna be a good one too. We're going to roast that boar Cody killed the other day and serve it up with beer."

"Along with the crate of Jim Beam I found in Mason's trailer," Clete added, leaning forward. "Guess who don't get any of that either?"

Ralph gunned his engine and, with a screech of the brakes, the Ford flew across the lot toward the main driveway.

Walter shook his head ruefully. "Suddenly I'm *persona non grata* at the camp, that it? After all I've done for everybody too." He started his engine, and eased the Tundra out of the lot to follow Ralph down the driveway.

Sitting by the window with the barrel of his Ruger carbine poking out the window, Cody grinned. "We've got a thirty minute drive back to the Alaculsy Valley. Maybe the lure of roast pig and whiskey might get something out of you by then!"

CHAPTER 2

He dreamed a never-ending dream, so real that if it were not for the crow, he would not have believed it was a dream at all. It sat perched on his shoulder, its piercing black eyes the color of obsidian, and talked to him through the hole in his head, whispering things that made no sense.

All the while, a fire raged deep in his mind, its searing heat so painful that he could barely think. Yet through the pain, the dream persisted.

He was chief of a powerful tribe that lived in a lush green valley. A river ran through it, and his camp was built to one side of its banks. It was a time of war. Through the mists, an army presented itself before him. Soldiers charged through the valley, armed with pistols and rifles, even axes. But he and his tribe were too strong for them. One after another, they were slain until their bodies stacked up in mounds, and their blood spilled into the river so that it turned the color of wine.

But the crow wouldn't let him rest. It urged him to leave the valley, to seek out even more armies to destroy, telling him not to stop until the whole world knelt before his feet.

That's impossible, he told the crow. *How can one man rule the world?*

The world as you know it is dead, the crow replied. *This is a new beginning. And in the beginning, everything is possible. Now forward, don't stop until the entire world submits to your rule. This is your destiny.*

He did as the crow commanded, and marched out of the valley, conquering all who challenged him until he lost count of how many lay dead before him. Exhausted, he knelt by a bloody pool and caught sight of his own reflection. A man he didn't recognize stared back at him. Other than for a strip of hair that ran down the center of his head, the rest of his scalp was shaved. Above his right temple was a small hole, its entrance caked in blood.

Who is that? he asked the crow. *Is it me?*

It is who you will become, said the crow. *Once you reach out and grasp your destiny.*

This made no sense to him.

When will all this fighting end? he asked. *I grow weary of it.*

Not until you have defeated the man who has caused you this pain. Only then will the fire that rages inside your head be quelled.

He wanted this more than anything else in the world.

What is the name of this man? he cried out. *I will seek him out and destroy him!*

The crow dipped its beak into the hole in his head again and whispered a name that echoed around the chambers of his mind.

His name is Walter...Walter...Walter...

CHAPTER 3

Things returned to normal quickly at Camp Eastwood. While security measures remained strict, without any imminent threat, the additional observation posts that had been setup at either end of the valley were abandoned and work started in earnest again on the farm. There was plenty to do. Even though North Georgia winters were relatively mild, Walter was keen to make the most of the long summer days and have the farm up and running as soon as possible.

Now that the Bentons had moved out, the farmhouse bedrooms had been taken over by the Georgians as originally planned. Marcie and Simone moved into the largest, the mid-sized bedroom was allocated to Jenny and Laura, while Billy Bingham got the smallest one at the end of the hall.

Though pleased with their new dwellings, they missed their lives underneath the stand of apple trees. Sleeping on his own, Billy missed it the most. He'd gotten used to chatting to the others through the thin nylon walls of his tent before drifting off to sleep at nights.

"Come wintertime, you won't miss it," Marcie comforted him. She stood with him by her window, gazing down at the field below. "There'll be a hard frost on the ground and gales blowing. You'll be grateful to be in your snug, warm bed."

"I guess I'll get used to it," Billy said, a little wistfully.

"Will you still say goodnight to us?" Laura asked. She had just entered the room to join the two.

Billy wheeled around to face her. "Probably not," he said, his cheeks reddening.

Marcie stifled a smile. "How about you come in and say goodnight to everyone before going to bed? Maybe we can't talk like before, but the most important thing is that we're all in shouting distance of each other. You know, in case the boogie man comes."

Laura shook her head emphatically, her golden curls tossing from side to side. "Oh no, the boogie man won't come here. He's way too scared of Ralph."

This time, Marcie allowed herself to smile fully. "See how lucky we are?" She cackled. "We've got our very own monster to drive away all the others!"

What was missed by all at the camp, however, were the Bentons. Over the duration of their brief stay at the Alaculsy Valley, many new friendships had formed and the place felt a little empty without them. Always fond of an adrenaline rush, Cody craved for the daily excitement of the war committee. He'd learned a lot from Walter and Ned Granger during that time. Military planning involved more than he'd previously thought. Both the Snake's Head and Blitzkrieg operations had been meticulously planned.

Emma suffered too. While she remained good friends with Greta and Maya, she missed Colleen Murphy. She admired the Irishwoman's mental toughness and dry sense of humor. The day they parted back at Camp Benton, the two had hugged each other tightly and vowed to visit one another soon. However, both knew that, in these times, that wouldn't be for quite a while.

***

Under Marcie and Billy's guidance, the farm continued to improve. Each morning, the Georgians, often helped by

Emma, Greta, and Maya, would rise at dawn and begin their work. In one of the fields at the back of the farm, both hoop houses were quickly constructed. Inside them, they built raised beds and covered them with plastic mulch. Once the soil was ready, beets, carrots, spinach, and turnips would be seeded from the supply Fred had brought with him from Maysville. On the next scavenge run, some type of shade fabric would need to be sourced in order to protect newly-planted crops from the summer heat.

The team planned to next work on a disused three-acre field at the very end of the Eastwood property and grow cereals, starting off with corn. Inside one of the work sheds, Simone discovered a small plow that fit onto the back of the tractor. It made sense to make the most of the machinery, as Walter had warned everyone not to count on fuel lasting forever.

There were grander plans afoot as well. Billy had brought several books from his family farm. One in particular his father used to reference constantly: *The Resilient Farm and Homestead*. Its philosophy was based on permaculture principles, something Marcie had never heard of before. After having seen how wonderful Willow Spring Farm had turned out, she was happy to learn. Pretty soon, she could be found late afternoons sitting in the herb garden under the shade of the trellis with her nose buried in the book.

She was fascinated by what she read. Though based on age-old organic farming principles, permaculture was far more than that. It was about transforming dull, worn landscapes, that might be otherwise overlooked by farmers as unworthy land, into beautiful, nutrient-dense ecosystems through rapid topsoil formation, remineralization, and fertility management.

A core tenet of permaculture was a zonation concept that laid out the landscape according to frequency and ease of use. The zones were numbered from 0 to 5, and made a series of concentric rings moving out from a center point, where there was the most need for attention, to where practically no attention was required at all. In this way, energy and water needs could be reduced while still creating a harmonious, sustainable environment.

Zone 0 was the home shelter. In their case, the farmhouse. The tiny herb pots Billy's mother had grown were brought in from the garden and placed along the window ledge behind the kitchen sink. A system to sprout and ferment foods was planned for the small annex room once the appropriate materials could be sourced. In the kitchen, additional bins were put in place so that all food waste could be used in outdoor compost bins.

Zone 1 was the area closest to the house. Other than planting a few salad crops, the vegetable and herb garden already fit their needs perfectly. Billy and Simone reassembled Willow Spring's cold frames in one corner, then set up a propagation area and a worm compost bin for the kitchen waste. At the same time, the rest of the Georgians got to work planting strawberries and raspberry beds along either side of the garden path.

Zone 2 was for perennial plants that required little maintenance other than occasional weed control. It was where Billy and Marcie planned on planting a "food forest," one that mimicked a natural forest system where plants and animals interacted, naturally supporting each other, and, once setup, required minimal human intervention. It would have cover crops, shrubs, and trees of various sizes, as well as creepers and vines to create a "stacking effect" with the various plants growing at different heights.

The two moved the chicken and rabbit pens over to this zone. Their droppings would provide fertilizer for plants, and control insect and weed populations. Soon nitrates and pesticides would run out in the world. By then, it would be advisable to have the farm running on more age-old principles.

Zone 3 was the area where the main crops would be grown, such as corn, wheat, and pumpkin. Seeing as most of the farmland had previously been used for grazing, it would take a while to develop, even with the plow. Once established, though, minimal care would be required, such as watering and weed control.

Zone 4 was for collecting firewood and gathering wild foods, like nuts, mushrooms, and native fruits. Beyond that, Zone 5 was the rarely visited wildlife areas surrounding the homestead.

Billy noted how the use of Zone 5 had changed since the pandemic. Lifting his head from the book he and Marcie were studying together one afternoon, he pointed up to the densely forested slopes of the Alaculsy Valley. "Now that deer and boar are our main sources of protein, we spend more time in Zone 5 than when this book was written," he mused. "Sometime soon, we're going to have to think about keeping more livestock. It only makes sense."

Marcie looked at him approvingly. "That's a wise head sitting on such young shoulders. You know, if I believed in such a thing, I'd say this wasn't your first time walking this Earth."

Billy looked at her in confusion, then returned to reading the book. Marcie smiled. She was seventy-two years old. Only the good Lord knew how many years she had left on this Earth. In that time, she intended to do all she could to help transform Eastwood into a paradise.

CHAPTER 4

When he awoke, his body was covered in a thick sweat. Above his right temple, his head throbbed painfully. He opened his eyes to find himself in a forest clearing, lying flat on his back. Above him, sunlight flickered through the leaves, and a warm breeze swept across his face.

A series of thoughts tumbled through his mind, one after another.

Where am I? Why am I in such pain? Then…*Who am I?*

Behind him, he heard movement. He turned his head to see a figure walk toward him. "Who's that?" he cried out, his voice parched and hoarse.

"*Shh…*" a voice said softly. "Don't shout. You never know who's around." The figure squatted beside him. It was a big man with sloping shoulders, a round face, and dark, curly hair. A set of dull brown eyes gazed gently down at him. "Finally, you're awake. Oh man, do you have any idea how long you've been out?"

"Why, what happened?" Instinctively, he raised his hand up to the right side of his head and could feel a bandage covering it. "What's wrong with me?"

"You got shot when the gang stormed the lodge." The man let out a low sob. "Th-they killed everyone, Chris."

Chris? The name meant nothing to him. He had no idea who the man staring down at him was either. "Who are you?" he asked.

The man blinked at him in surprise. "It's Mark. Don't you remember?"

"No."

Chris looked around him. At the edge of the clearing, a dark brown tent stood in the shade between two pine trees. Some camping gear was stacked neatly to one side of it, while on the other side was a one-ring camping stove. In front of the tent, a tarpaulin sheet had been laid out.

"You say we were attacked. Why?" he asked. "And what are we doing here in the forest?"

Mark's face took on a look of concern. "Don't you remember anything? The pandemic? Our survivor group…I mean *your* survivor group? You were our leader."

"No. Nothing."

"Shit, I think your injury has affected your memory."

It was the first thing that made any sense to Chris since he'd awakened. "Tell me what happened," he urged Mark. "Something recent, like when we were attacked. It might help me remember."

Mark drew a deep breath. When he spoke, his words gushed out in a garbled torrent that Chris had difficulty following.

"Th-they came during the night. James and Tim were on guard duty. They were killed first. They shot you next, when you came out of your trailer. You didn't stand a chance."

"And you?"

"I was in the trailer farthest away. By the time I came out, there was nothing I could do, so I slipped around the back and ran into the forest. Once I was sure no one was following me, I stopped and hid. I was only wearing shorts and sandals, I had no idea what else to do. Luckily, I had my Sig, though." Mark pulled a pistol from out of a holster by his waist and showed it to Chris.

Nothing came back to him. The only thing he understood was that he had been shot in the head, that it was the reason he remembered nothing. "Then what?"

Mark gulped again then continued. "I crept back to the edge of the forest to see what was going on. That's when they killed Eddy."

"Eddy…" Chris said slowly. Another name that meant nothing to him.

"He was your second-in-command. After they killed him, they dumped him and the rest of the bodies in the woods, real close to where I was hiding." Mark shook his head. "Oh man, you were so lucky. I was about to leave when I heard you moan. I couldn't believe it. I put you over my shoulder and carried you into the forest. We've been camped here ever since."

Mark pointed behind him to the tent. "See? I've been busy. The next morning, I took a car from one of the lakeside houses and drove into Ocoee Town to fetch supplies. The tent, food, water." He pointed at Chris's head. "Medical supplies too."

"How long have I been unconscious?"

"Eight days, Chris. Eight long days. To be honest, I wasn't sure if you would ever wake up. Every night I brought you into the tent. In the mornings, I carried you out again to rest here in the shade. I thought a little sunlight might help you wake up." Mark smiled. "Perhaps I was right."

Eight days. No wonder his dreams had seemed endless. For a brief moment, the image of a crow with piercing black eyes appeared in his mind's eye. A voice spoke to him, as clearly as Mark's. *Your destiny awaits you. Grasp it now!*

He bolted upright and clutched Mark's arm. "You say I was a leader. Tell me more. I need to know who I am."

Mark stood up. "First I'm going to fetch the medicine bag and take a look at your injury, then I'll do my best to explain." He headed over to the tent and returned moments later, carrying a canvas tote bag. Placing it on the ground, he knelt beside Chris again and began removing the bandage from his head. Once it was off, he leaned forward and inspected the wound. "That's better," he said, after a few moments. "It's healing nicely."

From the bag, he took out a lady's vanity mirror and handed it to Chris. Chris raised it to his head and took his first look at the injury that had put him in a coma for over a week.

The bullet had penetrated his skull an inch above his right temple, creating a perfectly-shaped hole about the diameter of a AA battery. A dark-colored scab had formed over it, and around the area, the skin was mottled and discolored.

There was no exit wound. Somewhere inside his skull, a piece of dull metal sat lodged in his brain. Chris focused his attention on the area. A strange sensation pulsed back at him, a fiery red heat signaling rage and fury.

He lowered the mirror. "The wound has healed. Nothing can be done about the bullet now. It'll remain there for as long as I live."

Mark smiled. "You've survived. That's all that counts." He rummaged around the bag and pulled out a pair of scissors and a roll of adhesive dressing.

Chris shook his head. "No need for that now the scab has formed. Just clean up the area around the wound."

Mark scrabbled around the bag some more and produced a pack of sterile pads and a bottle of hydrogen peroxide. He opened the bottle, poured a few drops onto one of the pads, and began scrubbing around the wound. The blood had caked hard against Chris's scalp and it took some effort. When Mark was done, he chucked the pad away and packed everything back into the bag.

Chris picked up the mirror and took another look. Though clean, the skin around the wound was abraded and discolored, forming a second, light-pink circle around the bullet hole.

He lowered the mirror. "Now, tell me everything I need to know. About the pandemic, about me and you. About the man who shot me. Slowly this time."

Mark puffed out his cheeks. "Brace yourself. You've no idea how crazy the world has become."

For the next hour, he filled Chris in about his previous life. He explained that they had met in Knoxville shortly after a deadly virus called vPox had decimated the country. The two had been among the survivors. Chris had started his own group and had recruited Mark and several others to come with him to the Cohutta. A few days after they arrived, a gang had attacked the lodge, and only Mark, Chris, and a lady called Liz, who the gang had released unharmed, had survived.

The talk of a pandemic that had almost wiped out humanity bewildered Chris. It seemed too incredible to believe, and he wondered whether he was still dreaming. This time, though, no armies presented themselves before him. No rivers ran the color of wine, and he had to accept that this was all real.

"This other woman...Liz. Where is she?" he asked.

"Mason, the leader of the gang, let her go. I think she went and joined the Benton group."

Chris raised an eyebrow. "The Benton group?"

"They live up at the YMCA camp." Mark hesitated. "Chris, it's complicated. Mason stormed their camp and took it over. A few days later, the Bentons took it back again."

"And the man who shot me. Mason. Where is he now?"

"He was killed when the Bentons took back the camp."

Chris frowned. "How do you know that?"

"I don't know for sure. But his gang got wiped out. Those that survived were executed down at the lake." Mark smiled. "I've gotten pretty good at spying on people lately."

Chris felt a sense of frustration rise in him. It appeared that the man who had destroyed his group and almost killed him was dead. There would be no way for him to exact revenge.

He was about to reply when the fragment of a memory floated across his mind. He stood outside a trailer in a large field. A small crowd gathered around him while he and a black man fought. He felt an intense dislike for this man, hatred even, yet this couldn't be Mason. Mason had shot him, not fought him in unarmed combat.

"Before I was shot, I fought somebody. A black man. Who is he?"

Mark looked surprised. "You remember Walter?"

Walter! That was the name the crow had given him.

Chris stared at Mark, his eyes burning. "Yes, Walter. Tell me everything you know about him."

CHAPTER 5

Walter was keen to get started on his micro hydro system. However, his training as a military engineer taught him how important it was to be suitably prepared before embarking on such a project. With that in mind, the first thing he needed to do was to setup a workshop where he could store his tools and materials.

Nosing around the farm's many outbuildings, he found one that suited his needs perfectly, a thirty-foot barn that had a concrete laid floor and a sturdy corrugated tin roof. Previously, it had been used for storing feed, and dozens of sacks of soybean and cornmeal were stacked up against the back wall. After fetching Cody, the two spent a couple of hours clearing the place out.

Cody found an old wheelbarrow and began transferring the feed to another building. It would be used for feeding the farm's livestock, such as the chicken and rabbits.

"Who knows? If Marcie and Billy don't get everything up and running at the farm on time, we might end up using it ourselves," Walter joked as Cody wheeled out the last of the fifty-pound bags. "We can line everyone up at a trough and pour it in."

Cody grinned. "Mmm, delicious. Please sir, may I have some more?"

Though morning, without electricity, it was gloomy in the workshop. It would remain that way until the micro hydro was built. For the moment, Walter intended to set up his workbench by the barn entrance to get as much natural light as he could.

After a final sweep of the floor, the two started transferring the materials Walter had taken with him from Knoxville that had been stored in Pete's trailer for safekeeping. One was a small cardboard box with the words "R/E MAGNETS" hand-scrawled on it.

Cody picked it up. "What's in this?" he asked, surprised by how heavy the box was.

"They're rare-earth magnets," Walter told him. "Before leaving Knoxville, I snuck home and picked up a few things from my workshop. They were part of a project I was playing around with before the pandemic struck." He tapped the side of his head with his finger. "Just to keep the gray matter exercised. It never occurred to me I might need to use them for real."

Cody still looked puzzled. "Yes, but what are they for, exactly?"

"I'll use them to convert a car alternator to what's known as a 'permanent magnet alternator', a PMA. It's the most efficient way of harnessing natural energy sources such as wind and hydro."

Cody knew a little about car engines – he'd had a friend who rebuilt muscle cars, and had occasionally helped him. An alternator was used to charge the battery. Without it, the battery would quickly drain, and the vehicle would become inoperable.

"Why do you need to convert it, though? Won't it work just fine as it is?"

Walter shook his head. "A car's alternator is designed to harness the energy from a high RPM engine. The waterwheel I intend building will turn far slower. To draw sufficient power from it, I'll need to modify the alternator."

This was the first time Cody had heard exactly what type of hydro power Walter intended building. "A waterwheel? Sounds cool. Where you going to install it?"

"There's a creek at the southeast corner of the camp that suits our needs perfectly. It's got enough water flow to drive the wheel." Walter opened his A4 notebook, which he carried everywhere these days, and plucked the pen clipped to the top. "Now, I need to finish my list. After lunch, we'll make a run to Dalton City and get more supplies. With a bit of luck, we should find everything we need to build this thing."

Two hours later, Walter, along with a heavily-armed Cody, Emma, and Clete, left camp, leaving Ralph, Pete, Greta, and Simone on guard. Though Mason was dead, Walter didn't like leaving a depleted force behind, but heading out of the valley without plenty of firepower was plain reckless these days. Besides, by now, Marcie, Fred, and Billy were well-trained in case the camp came under attack. Soon, though, they would need to bolster their numbers, and the previous day Pete had volunteered to go off on another recruitment drive. Walter had told him to hold off another couple of days, cryptically telling him there might be no need for it.

Arriving at Dalton City, their first stop was Home Depot. The huge building was pitch-black inside, and all four switched on their flashlights. Though the store looked like it had been ransacked recently, Walter hoped he would find the tools he needed. The items he required wouldn't be at the top of most survivors' lists.

Consulting his notebook, he scattered Cody, Clete, and Emma around the warehouse to source the items. In short order, two power drills, a cordless jigsaw, a carpenter's plane, and several handsaws went into his cart. Next in went a set of Phillips and flathead screwdrivers, quickly followed by tape measures, c-clamps, pliers, wrenches, levels, and squares. In a second cart, pushed by Emma, two large machine-operated saws were carefully placed, a chop saw and a miter saw.

The micro hydro would need tools to configure the electronics. Clete soon found several reels of electrical cord, wire strippers, and a set of Allen keys.

"Excellent," Walter said, chucking them into his cart.

From another section of the store, Cody returned with a four-hundred-piece mechanic's tool set. He placed it inside Emma's cart, trundling alongside Walter's.

"Right," Walter said to Cody and Clete, indicating to the now full shopping carts. "Why don't you two go load the truck. Emma, help me find where they keep the workbenches."

After a short search, the two found the section where they were stored. Walter decided to take two so that more than just him could work easily at the same time. He selected two sturdy wooden workbenches and, one at a time, he and Emma carried them outside.

Once they'd been loaded in the back of the Tundra, Walter examined his list again. Though they still had plenty of twenty-pound propane cylinders back at camp, Walter handed Cody the keys to his truck and sent him and Clete off to find more. The tanks were popular with survivors, who used them to run their camp stoves, and it made sense to be well-stocked.

"See if you can source some acetylene tanks too," he told them. "Might as well pick up some welding gear while we're here. You never know when it might come in useful."

While they were gone, Walter and Emma set about gathering the last of the items on the list. Walter selected an eighteen-horsepower propane generator needed for charging the power tools, then the two wheeled the cart to the area of the store where the welding equipment was kept.

Finally, they found the hardware department. Angling his flashlight around the shelves, Walter spotted some metal sheets, then a two-meter-long threaded metal rod along with its accompanying bolts.

"They'll do nicely," he said.

"What for?" Emma asked curiously as Walter placed the rod and bolts inside the cart.

"I'm going to use the rod as the axle for the waterwheel," he told her. "I just need to find the hubs to attach it to. We'll get them on the way home. Right, that's everything. Let's get out of here."

It took Cody and Clete over thirty minutes to get back. Walter and Emma were waiting outside for them on their return.

Clete hopped out the front passenger door. "We found a couple of acetylene tanks at a workshop on the outskirts of town," he informed Walter. "The propane was harder to find. We finally spotted a couple of tanks around the back of a grocery store."

Walter frowned. The cylinders were going faster than he thought.

"All right," he said after they loaded the last of the items into the Tundra's crammed load bed. "Let's get going. We've still one more stop to make."

On the way home, Walter headed down a residential street, where several cars sat in the driveways of the homes. He drove slowly past until he found what he was looking for, then pulled up at the curb in front of a red Toyota Camry.

He looked around at his passengers. "Anybody here good at working on cars?"

"Been working on them all my life," Clete replied from the back seat. "Anytime I wasn't out hunting, drunk, or in the can, that is."

Walter pointed over to the Toyota. "You think you can pull the alternator out of that Camry? If you can, I left the tool set by the tailgate."

Clete opened his door. "Give me fifteen minutes," he said confidently.

"I'll need the serpentine belt for it too!" Walter called out after him, then winked at Cody. "Sure saves me from getting my hands dirty, don't it?"

Cody grinned. "I've worked on cars too. I just had the good sense not to boast about it."

"Yeah? So happens I need the two front wheel-bearing hubs out of the Camry too. Go grab a couple of wrenches from Clete and get to work."

Cody groaned. "Me and my big mouth." He opened his door and ambled over to where Clete had already popped the hood of the Camry.

Fifty minutes later, Walter's two workers returned. They placed the Camry's alternator, serpentine belt, and two wheel hubs in the truck bed. Cody's shirt was filthy, his hands covered in thick axle grease. Walter waved an old rag out the window. "Clean up before you get inside," he told him.

"That your way of saying thanks?" Cody grumbled, taking the rag from him. A trickle of sweat ran down the side of his face from his exertions. It hadn't been easy removing the wheel hubs. Clete had gotten the easier job.

"Nope," Walter chuckled. "It's my way of saying I like to keep this vehicle nice and clean."

On the journey home, Walter considered the propane situation. It wasn't going to last much longer. A thought struck him, one so simple he wondered why he hadn't thought of it before. Once he'd installed the waterwheel and the camp had electricity, he'd talk to Ned Granger about it. If things worked out the way he hoped, Camp Eastwood would soon have a big enough supply to last them several years.

CHAPTER 6

The following morning, Chris woke up headache free. He'd had no gory dreams, and awoke from a deep, dark nothingness as if he'd been under anaesthesia the entire night. All that remained of his injury was a dull pressure at the center of his head. It was a peculiar sensation, like that part of his mind no longer belonged to him. Something whirred busily inside; he just had no idea what.

Though he'd lost weight, he hadn't been in the coma long enough for his muscles to atrophy significantly. The previous day, Mark had fed him cans of chicken soup heated on the camping stove. He regained his strength quickly. By that evening, he was eating regular meals alongside Mark.

After breakfast, he went for a long walk in the forest, accompanied by Mark. Later in the day, he did a more vigorous exercise, a twenty-minute session of martial arts *katas*, which he had no memory of ever doing, yet somehow he knew how to make the precise movements of the varied routine.

He came to view his lost memory as a jigsaw puzzle, one that he would slowly piece back together again. During the day, fragments would come to him in sudden, episodic flashes. They overpowered his senses. His normal vision disappeared, to be replaced by a sequence of events that played in his mind. Afterward, he would ask Mark questions about what he'd seen. Chris quickly recognized that Mark wasn't very bright, making understanding everything that much harder.

Mark seemed reluctant to talk about Walter too, stating only that after their fight, he'd left the group. Chris wasn't surprised by that.

"We fought, I beat him. He couldn't handle it."

Mark lowered his eyes. "Right. But see, some of the others left with him. It weakened the group, made it easy for Mason to storm the camp."

Chris stared at him, stunned. "Some of my people left to go with *Walter*?"

Mark nodded. Making his excuses, he wandered off, leaving Chris to dwell on what he'd said. His injury, the loss of his group—it was all down to Walter.

That evening, he experienced another of his memory flashes. Eating a plate of chili con carne over rice that Mark had prepared from a can, he froze, his fork halfway to his mouth as a new episode played in his head.

He lay on the ground outside a trailer, staring up at the sky. Walter stood over him, his fists clenched by his sides. Then Eddy appeared. He reached down and helped him to his feet. As he stared woozily around the crowd of shocked faces, Chris realized that it had been *him*, not Walter, who had lost the fight.

Beside him, he felt Mark shaking his shoulder. The sequence stopped, and his normal vision returned.

"Walter won the fight, not me," he said angrily. "Why didn't you tell me?"

"You remember?" Mark said, looking uncomfortable. "I was going to tell you, only I didn't see the point. It doesn't matter anyway. He got a lucky punch in, that's all."

The rage burning inside Chris grew even stronger. "I'm going to ask you one more time," he grated. "Where did Walter and the others go?"

"I-I told you, Chris, I don't know. I heard they went deeper into the Cohutta, that's all. Look, forget about Walter. He had nothing to do with what happened to you."

"Yes, he did!" Chris shouted. "You told me yourself. He stole my people and made it easy for Mason to—"

He stopped mid-sentence as a dark shadow fluttered across his peripheral vision and landed lightly on his shoulder. He turned to see the crow perched on it. It leaned over and whispered into the hole in his head.

Control yourself. Today you take the first steps in grasping your destiny. Listen carefully to what I say...

Once more, time slipped away.

When the vision ended and he came to his senses, Mark was looking at him anxiously. "You okay?" he asked.

Chris stared back at him, his eyes shining fiercely. "Fetch me some fresh razors and the medicine bag," he told him. "Today we make the change to mark our new beginning. From this day forward, our lives will never be the same."

Mark looked at him uncertainly. "What do you mean? I don't understand."

"Do as I say. You'll see soon enough."

When Mark returned, Chris took him over to the edge of the camp and squatted next to the small brook where he'd washed that morning. He instructed Mark to take out the vanity mirror and hold it up to his head.

While Mark did so, Chris began cutting his hair down to stubble, other than for a long strip he left down the middle of his head.

When it had all been shorn off, he handed Mark a razor and instructed him to shave the remaining stubble.

Mark scooped some water into his hands and wet Chris's head. Daubing shaving cream over it, he began shaving Chris's scalp, other than for the strip that ran from his forehead all the way to the base of his skull.

"Chris, why are you doing this?" Mark asked hesitantly. "I mean, I'm cool with it. I just want to know why."

Chris echoed the words the crow had told him. "This will be the mark of our tribe. One that will grow so powerful all others shall yield before it. It is time for warriors to rule the Earth again."

Mark grinned, his normally dull eyes shining. "Man, that is awesome!"

When he finished, Mark scooped some more river water into his hands and washed off Chris's scalp. Chris reached down into the medicine bag and took out the bottle of hydrogen peroxide and some cotton balls. He poured peroxide onto one of the pads and started applying it to his remaining strip of hair.

A short time later, he raised the mirror again and inspected himself. His entire head was shaved, other than for the bleached white strip down the middle.

He faced Mark. "How do I look?"

Mark grinned. "Like you're going to scare the hell out of people."

"That's the idea." Chris picked up the scissors and handed them to Mark. "Now…your turn."

CHAPTER 7

A white pickup truck approached the Harris Branch, driving north from the Georgia line. Reaching the clearing, it slowed, then drove off the road toward where a large oak tree stood, making a loud swishing sound as its wheels mowed through the high grasses.

Walter pulled the Tundra up beside where another vehicle had already arrived, a cream and tan Dodge Charger with Polk County Sheriff markings on the door. He got out and strolled over to where Sheriff Rollins leaned against the hood of his vehicle.

It had been three days since their brief talk in the Benton council room. This was the place and time the two had agreed to meet again.

"How goes it?" Walter asked after they shook hands. "Everyone happy to be back in their old surroundings?"

Rollins smiled. "Relieved more than anything else."

Walter looked at him expectantly? "And?"

"Well…things haven't improved at the lake. Gangs everywhere. I won't allow anyone out unless they're an armed group of three or more, and even then it's dangerous."

That day when Rollins had held Walter back at the office, the sheriff had asked him how he and his group might feel if the Bentons moved up the Alaculsy Valley to join them. It had surprised Walter. They had just spent the last few days plotting to defeat Mason and retake the camp. No sooner had they achieved that, and the sheriff was already thinking about leaving.

Rollins spent the next ten minutes explaining his reasoning. While the old YMCA camp had initially suited the Benton's needs, the area wasn't suitable to take their community to the next level. It was too heavily forested for any type of agriculture, and with the increasing activity around the lake, much of it hostile, Rollins doubted they could make it work as a long-term solution. "We're starting to feel hemmed in," he'd told Walter.

Having spent time in the Alaculsy Valley, the sheriff saw how beneficial it might be for the Bentons to move there. There was plenty of unclaimed farmland that would give them the opportunity to build a large, sustainable community. And, of course, having two groups living side by side would mean better security for all.

"Have you sounded things out with your people yet?" Rollins asked, staring at Walter keenly.

"I haven't made a formal proposal yet until we flesh a few things out, but I've talked to someone in private about it. How about you?"

"Likewise. It's a delicate situation. No point in proposing some ill-thought out plan that ends up pissing everyone off."

Walter nodded. "I'm confident I can get everyone on board. There's plenty of room in the valley, so long as the terms are carefully agreed." He smiled. "I think you'll have the harder time convincing your people to move from the Benton area."

"You're right. So far, I've only talked to Ned about it. We've spent a lot of time thinking this through. Ned's pretty sure he can convince Hank. The two go back a way."

"That's good. If Hank agrees, that gives your council a majority decision."

"True, but I'd like to have everyone on board. It's important that Mary and Bert agree to this too. The last thing we need is a schism in the camp where some of our people agree to go, while others elect to stay. That would defeat the whole purpose of the move. We need to strengthen our community, not weaken it." Rollins paused a moment. "To make this thing fly, we need to agree certain conditions in advance. Otherwise, I won't get it past the council."

Walter understood Rollins perfectly. This was a big undertaking on his part. From his military experience, he knew it didn't take much for people to lose confidence in their leadership. Even a small misstep could undermine it.

He had a good idea what was on Rollins's mind too. Like the sheriff, he also needed to be careful, and had spent many hours considering the main stumbling blocks to developing a joint community such as Rollins proposed.

He leaned back against the side of the Charger. "All right, Sheriff. Let's talk. See if we can't come up with something that works."

CHAPTER 8

One of the projects Billy's father had intended to pursue back at Willow Spring Farm had been to build a freshwater aquaculture system. Now it was on Billy's mind too. After carefully studying the relevant chapters in *The Resilient Farm and Homestead*, he sought Marcie out.

He found her at the end of the property, where she and her team were clearing the three-acre field close to where the hoop houses had been built. Over the past few days, the dormant grasses had been scythed and burnt in great big piles. When Billy arrived, Simone waved at him from behind the wheel of the tractor. It trundled slowly across the field, its plow tilling the soil with its heavy blades. He waved back, then hurried over to Marcie.

"Why would we want to build a pond?" she asked after Billy broached his idea with her. She pointed down at the Conassauga River, visible from where they stood. "Right there is a perfect freshwater system. It's got all the fish we need."

Billy lowered his head and began reading from the book he'd brought with him. *"There's more to permaculture than just a zonation concept. Its design principles allow for the radical transformation of terrain through large scale, earth moving projects, so long as the changes work in harmony with nature, not against it.*

Designed correctly, a freshwater aquaculture system can achieve greater overall protein production per square meter of water surface area than a land system. As well as protein, it provides a variety of medicinal plants, along with a steady supply of edible foods such as watercress, taro, water chestnuts, and spinach." He looked up from the book. "See? It will give us a constant supply of food all year round. And it'll be a fun place to hang out...you know, for the kids," he added earnestly.

Marcie stared at the solemn young boy, unable to suppress a smile. "Well, if it's somewhere for the *kids* to hang out, I don't suppose there's any harm in building one. I like the idea of growing medicinal plants too. It's something I know a little about."

Billy looked pleased. He snapped the book shut and grabbed her arm. "Come on, let's find Walter. We're going to need his help."

Though they looked everywhere, Walter was nowhere to be found. His pickup was missing too. At the med trailer that served as his and Greta's living quarters, Greta told the two he'd gone off for a few hours and would be back later that afternoon.

Marcie frowned. "Where did he go? He just went to Dalton City yesterday."

"He's not on a scavenging run. He's doing something completely different."

"Such as what? "

Greta hesitated. "I really couldn't tell you." She checked her watch. "Why don't you ask him when he gets back? He's due soon."

***

When Walter returned to camp, he found Billy waiting for him. He was sitting up on one of the sandbag parapets in the corner of the front yard where the vehicles parked. As soon as Walter cut the engine, Billy leapt down and ran over to him.

"Something on your mind?" Walter asked after getting out of the truck, noting the young boy's demeanor. His normal studious air was replaced by an animated expression, and he literally hopped from one foot to the other.

Billy grabbed Walter's arm and began dragging him away. "Come on," he said impatiently. "Me and Marcie have something important to tell you."

He took Walter around the back of the farmhouse and through the side gate that led into the herb garden. Sitting under the shade of the trellis, Marcie was reading a book. One of Willow Spring Farm's gardening books, Walter presumed. When either she or Billy weren't out in the field, it's what they generally did.

Their commitment to developing the farm impressed Walter. Despite his initial reservations about the bizarre array of people Pete had brought back from his recruitment mission, everyone had fit in surprisingly well. And having both the young and the old at Eastwood, from the chirpy eight-year-old Laura, to the irascible, seventy-three-year-old Fred, felt natural somehow. "Like a real community," Walter had commented to Greta the other night.

He sat down at the table, and Marcie immediately set about explaining the "freshwater aquaculture system" she and Billy proposed building. Occasionally referring to the book, she told him how it would provide a year-round source of protein for the camp, as well as vegetables, herbal medicines, and a host of other benefits. "Besides, it'll be a great place for the kids to hang out," she finished up by saying, glancing at Billy. "Somewhere they can splash about during the summer months."

"Sounds like a worthwhile project," Walter said. "You have my blessing to go ahead, if that's what you need of me."

Marcie glanced at Billy. "Our team can manage most of the work. One thing we'll need, though, is an excavator. The pond we intend building is too big to dig manually."

Walter considered this. "That involves another scavenging run. Once I've completed work on the micro hydro, we can take a look for one. I don't expect it'll be hard. Can't be too much demand for earth-movers these days."

"When will that be?" Billy asked anxiously. Like all children, he wanted to do things *now*.

"Oh, maybe in a week or so." Seeing the look of disappointment on the young boy's face, he added. "Or perhaps we can get our hands on a digger sooner than you think. There's big changes coming to Eastwood that should fit in perfectly with your plans."

Marcie's bushy gray eyebrows knitted together in a stern frown. "What are you talking about, Walter? Have you invited a construction crew to come and live with us here in the valley?"

Laughing, Walter stood up from the table. "Not quite, but close. I'm organizing a meeting this afternoon, where I'll be making an announcement. You'll find out soon enough." With that he sauntered out of the herb garden, leaving a puzzled Marcie and Billy behind.

CHAPTER 9

After lunch, Walter convened his meeting. It took place in the patio area of the herb garden where he'd talked to Marcie earlier. Even since the Bentons had departed, it continued to be the focal point for community gatherings. All were present other than Pete, who was keeping watch on top of the barn roof.

Although he'd told Rollins he was confident how his group would react to the news, now that the time had come, Walter felt a little nervous. Other than Greta, no one else knew about the plan. Despite Cody's best efforts, he hadn't been able to pry any information from him on their return to the Alaculsy Valley that day.

"I met with Sheriff Rollins this morning," he started off by saying. "He has a proposal for us. One that would entirely change the dynamics at this camp." Leaning against one side of the wrought-iron trellis, he spotted Cody nudging Ralph in the ribs. Both men were listening intently.

"Now that the Bentons have gotten through the first phase of their survival, they see that the YMCA camp isn't well suited to their needs going forward. While the fishing and hunting is excellent, there's no arable land nearby. Unless they intend remaining a 'hunter/scavenger' community forever, they need to find someplace else to move soon, somewhere that supports agriculture and the rearing of livestock. Right now, the sheriff is weighing his choices…" Walter let his voice drift off, giving time for people to see the direction he was taking.

Clete was the first to grasp his meaning. "So when are the Bentons coming up to the valley?" he chirped, tugging at his scrawny beard.

Walter smiled. "No flies on you, Mr. Hillbilly. Yes, that was the purpose of our discussion. The Alaculsy Valley is under consideration. For us, I think it makes sense. There's plenty of room, and with what we just experienced with Mason, it will improve our security situation tremendously. I doubt Mason will be the last bandit we encounter." He paused briefly. "While I see it as a win/win situation, whether you agree or not is what we need to discuss now."

"Where would they set up their camp?" Ralph asked, staring at Walter. "You intend that they merge with our group, or set up somewhere close by?"

Territorial considerations had been the very first item on Walter and Rollins's agenda. It would determine how the overall camp structure was run - as one, or as two separate entities. This had been a potentially contentious issue. Thankfully, both men shared a similar vision.

Walter nodded at Ralph appreciatively. "Another excellent question from the Atlanta contingent."

Clete grinned. "Who said us jailbirds were as thick as two short planks? All right, Walter, spit it out. What terms did you agree with the sheriff?"

"Nothing in stone," Walter replied hastily. "That wouldn't be right without agreement amongst all of us. We did discuss some basic principles, though. The camps would remain distinct entities, with their own boundaries, leadership, and rules. However, a council would be setup to work on communal projects and other vital issues that are in the interests of both camps."

"Such as security," Ralph said.

"Exactly. Security duties would be integrated between the camps. The 'War Committee,' as it was previously known during our battle with Mason, would become the 'Alaculsy Valley Security Council.'"

"Where do they intend setting up their new camp?" Cody asked.

"I proposed we let them stay at the Jonson property. We don't use it, and it's close enough where people from both camps can meet easily."

Cody nodded. "Makes sense if they're close by. It makes security arrangements easier."

Half a mile south of the Eastwood camp was another farm that, according to the mailbox, belonged to a family called the Jonsons. Though there were several outbuildings, it had no farmhouse. Whoever had tended the property had lived somewhere else - perhaps in Old Fort, the nearest town.

Walter glanced at Emma. From her wide smile, he knew that she was delighted with his proposal.

"I know that during the Bentons' time with us, many friendships were forged. Our success in defeating Mason only made them stronger."

"What else did you two discuss?" a harsh, crackling voice spoke out. It was Fred. He sat in his wheelchair at the back of the group. Eric, arms folded, leaned against the back of the chair. "Agreements like this can get more complicated than you think. Problem is, sometimes you don't figure that out until afterward."

"That was more or less it," Walter replied. "I don't know what everyone else thinks, but I believe we should keep this simple. Sure, we could build a long list of cleverly-worded rules that take into account every conceivable situation, but people will be just as clever at interpreting them to suit their purposes."

"Hear, hear!" Greta said, sitting next to Walter. "So long as we agree to the principles of solidarity and common purpose between our two camps, we'll do just fine."

Fred nodded. "I agree. Many years ago, I ran a small real estate company in Maysville. Mainly rental and leasing type stuff. The tax code and federal regulations used to break my heart. If I wasn't careful, I risked breaking some damn law I'd never heard of. All well and good for the corporations who had a department to handle that stuff. For a small business owner like me, it was a nightmare."

Walter smiled. "Let's hope we never return to those days. If we keep the politicians out of things, we'll do just fine." He gazed around the group, pleased by everyone's reaction. "All right. It's time to vote on the matter. All in favor of allowing the Bentons to move in beside us at the Jonson property, raise their hands."

Around the patio, all arms immediately shot up.

"Excellent," Walter said with satisfaction. "Now it's up to Sheriff Rollins to convince his people. Somehow, I don't think things will go quite as smoothly for him."

"Why? Hasn't he discussed it with them yet?" Emma asked.

Walter shook his head. "No, and some in their group may not want to leave the Benton area. After all, it's where many were born and raised. The sheriff thought it best to agree on things with us first, hence all the secrecy." He smiled wryly. "Boy, would I like to be a fly on the wall for that meeting. He's got a tough sell."

***

In the Benton council room, Sheriff Rollins stared across the table at three shocked faces. Only Ned Granger, who had been privy to Rollins's negotiations with Walter, looked calm.

"John, we've only just got back our camp! Now you want us to vacate it already?" Bert Olvan said, his face registering a mixture of incredulity and anger.

"And losing several good men in the process," Mary Sadowski added, both sides of her mouth tucked down in a stiff grimace. "I'll say this for you, John. You never cease to surprise me."

Rollins drew in his breath. "Look, this camp has been perfect for our needs, until now. Yes, we've got excellent facilities and the lake at our disposal. The problem is, we're surrounded by dense forest. In order for us to progress as a community, we need open land where we can grow crops and tend animals. That's impossible here."

"It's a pity the farm down at the Baptist church has been taken," Henry Perter said. "Maybe we should have claimed it. It's only a mile from here."

Rollins shook his head. "Too impractical, Hank. We would have had to leave guards there each night. Even then, it would have most likely been overrun. No, we need to move somewhere that we can defend as an entire group."

"Like where?" Olvan asked. "All the good farms on Benton's west side are already taken. Folk have been pouring in there from practically every city in Tennessee."

Rollins stole a quick glance at Ned Granger. "There's plenty of room at the Alaculsy Valley. Walter tells me we're welcome to build a camp next to theirs."

"What! And leave the Benton area?" Olvan thundered, his big frame shuddering with anger. "Hell no. I'll never agree to that!"

Mary Sadowski glared at Rollins. "John, you've been holding out on us. That's why you kept Walter back the other day. It had nothing to do with camp communications, did it?"

Rollins stared back at her, slightly embarrassed. "No, it didn't. I felt there was no point in raising this subject unless the Eastwoods were agreeable to us settling there. Otherwise, what would be the point? This morning I had a meeting with Walter. He told me he's confident his group will agree to it."

Scowling, Mary turned to Granger. "How about you, Ned? Were you involved in these negotiations?"

Arms folded across his chest, Granger shook his head.

"But you knew about them, didn't you?" Mary pressed.

"Yes, I knew," Granger replied. He unfolded his arms and leaned forward at the table, looking directly into Mary's eyes. "In my opinion, it's our best option right now. The land in the valley is excellent. We can plant crops there, and raise cattle and all sorts of livestock that will allow us to build a robust, sustainable community." He paused a moment to reflect. "Like many soldiers, I've studied military history all my life, but I'm also a student of general history. If you look back at how societies have developed throughout the ages, you'll find most were built on open, fertile land – or, at least, the ones that thrived did. Take Mesopotamia, for example, the cradle of civilization. It's where wheat was first planted as a cereal crop, and where goats, sheep, and pigs were first domesticated. If we intend to thrive as a community, we need to move from here. Of that, I'm certain. The Alaculsy Valley is our best option."

"You plan on becoming a goat herder, Ned?" Mary asked dryly. "Or a pig farmer?"

Granger shrugged. "I like hunting for meat. But sooner or later, we'll need farmers amongst us. Mark my words."

For the next twenty minutes, the discussion continued while everyone had their say. Finally, the conversation died down.

Rollins looked around the table. "Well, I think everyone's said their piece. Now all we need to do is vote. All in favor of the Benton survivors' group move to the Alaculsy Valley, raise their hands."

CHAPTER 10

In their trailer, Walter and Greta lay in bed. It was late evening, and the two were discussing the events of the day.

"You can't believe how delighted Emma is with the news," Greta was saying. "She became very close with Colleen while she was here." She glanced at Walter. "I know how happy you are about them coming here too."

Walter nodded. "If we're going to build a long-term, sustainable community in the valley, security is paramount. The addition of the Bentons will make things far safer. Safety in numbers, they say, so long as they're the *right* numbers. Like I told everyone earlier, Mason may be dead, but he's not the only one of his ilk. Rest assured, more like him will eventually show up here. We need to be prepared for them."

"True. Seems like no matter how much society has shrunk, there are still those who want to take away what others have. I just don't understand that mentality."

"The bubonic plague killed over half of Europe. It never stopped any war, or at least, not for long. There's always someone spoiling for a fight. Like it or not, it's in man's nature."

Greta sighed. "Sometimes I can't help but wonder if there's something inherently evil in man. It's why people have argued in favor of the social contract over the ages."

Walter looked at her. "The social contract? What's that?"

Greta smiled. "Believe it or not, before I decided to become a nurse, I studied philosophy. A fellow named Thomas Hobbes came up with the theory that, while everyone is entitled to freedom, people have no choice but to give some of that freedom up to a ruler or some type of governing authority."

"Why? I thought those philosophers valued freedom above everything else."

"Not all. In Hobbes's case, he argued that absent any political order, individuals are bound only by their consciences, and as we saw with Mason, that's not always a good thing. Peoples' 'state of nature,' as he called it, allows many to do bad things as well as good."

"No doubt, but we know from history that rulers aren't always good either. They rape and pillage, and lead their people into senseless wars."

"True, but Hobbes argued that even a despotic ruler is better than no rule at all. That without the rule of law, life would be 'brutish and short'...or words to that effect."

Walter mulled this over. "If we need rules, no matter how few, I guess *someone* has to impose them." He smiled. "Perhaps I should give being a despotic ruler a shot. Who knows? Could be fun."

Greta curled up closer to him, stretching one of her long legs over his. "Despotic ruler isn't your style. Now, a benevolent ruler, *a philosopher king*, such as Plato argued for in *The Republic*, that I could see."

"A philosopher king? You intrigue me. How does that play go down?"

Greta laughed. "I've opened a can of worms, haven't I? A philosopher king is one who rules his people with the purest of motives, one who makes decisions that are in the best interest of his people rather than his own."

"I guess I could do that." Walter grinned. "So long as I'm enjoying myself while I'm at it."

Greta shook her head. "I'm afraid not. The philosopher king is a wisdom-lover who spurns Earthly delights and must live a simple, aesthetic life so as not to become seduced by his own powers."

"What, no harem? Grapes dangled over my mouth by naked ladies while I'm rubbed with essential oils? Plato, you suck!"

Greta's hand rose up his leg, grabbing a delicate part of his anatomy. "Go down the harem route, and you'll end up a eunuch. Got that?" With a sudden twist of her hips, she sat up on top of him, straddling his waist. "How about I rule *you* for the next while? That can be fun too."

Walter stared up at her. "Rule the hell out of me. I don't mind."

CHAPTER 11

Three days later, the Bentons made their move up to the Alaculsy Valley. It had taken some work to make it happen. The first time around, the council's decision hadn't been unanimous. While Henry Perter had voted in favor of the move, both Bert Olvan and Mary Sadowski had been steadfast in their refusal, and it had taken the sheriff's casting vote to pass the motion.

Rollins's fears about a schism had been prescient. Immediately after the vote, Sadowski stood up from the table and stormed out of the room. Olvan had been more composed, but left too, intimating that he and Mary might remain at the camp if they could persuade enough in the group to stay with them.

It took the rest of the day to convince the two objectors on the soundness of the plan, and the importance of presenting a unified front when they broke the news to the rest of the group. This was a dangerous world they inhabited. People's lives were literally at stake.

Reluctantly, and a little sullenly, by late evening, first Olvan was swayed, then a very bitter Mary Sadowski. The vote was retaken, and a unanimous decision placed into the council's logbook, Mary's normally neat handwriting barely legible as she recorded the decision with a trembling hand.

Things moved swiftly after that. At breakfast the following morning, the announcement was made by Rollins. Echoing the council's initial reaction the previous day, shocked faces stared at each other around the dining hall, and there was a flurry of complaints and arguments. Many people had lived in the Benton area all their lives. While the Alaculsy Valley was only a forty-minute drive away, in these times, it felt like another world.

Though not from Benton, Jonah Murphy had balked at the idea. "I risked me bleedin' neck helping to take back this place, now we're just going to pack up and leave?" he fumed to his wife and their friend, Monica Jeffries, who all sat together at the same table. "And what will the fishing be like in this Alli-coolly Valley? Poxy, I bet. We came to Benton because of the lake."

"*You* came here because of the lake," Colleen reminded him. "I came to join a survivor community. Besides, I'm sure there'll be plenty of good fishing in the valley. Both the Conassauga and Jack's River run right by the Eastwood camp. Isn't that so, Monica?"

Monica nodded. "Before the pandemic, Jack's River was a popular spot for trout fishing. Charles took the kids up there on several occasions. I think you'll love it there."

"You sure?" Jonah asked doubtfully. Unlike the other two, he'd never been to the valley. When the Benton camp had been taken over by the bandit, Mason Bonner, he'd remained as a spy.

"Totally," Monica assured him. "Just wait and see."

Her comments pacified Jonah somewhat. Monica's husband had been a keen angler before the pandemic took him and her children. Though he'd never met the man, Jonah thought of him as a kindred spirit.

After some more quibbling, the thought of catching a few fifteen-inch rainbow trout finally brought Jonah around to the idea. Likewise, the majority of the Bentons reluctantly agreed how advantageous it would be to move out of the thick forest to a place where their community could progress to the next level. Joining the Eastwoods, who had already proved themselves in battle, only strengthened the argument.

Despite some grumblings, most people prepared for the move with a sense of anticipation, and soon everyone was busy packing their gear. The council were anxious to move right away. Partly, because Rollins was a little afraid that people might change their minds, but more simply, once the decision had been made, there wasn't much point in hanging around.

Seventy-two hours later, on a fresh July morning, they were gone.

***

It was an exciting moment for the Eastwoods when the long line of Benton vehicles showed up in the valley. Jenny and Laura, stationed at the hilltop lookout that morning, excitedly broke the news over the radio when the trucks trundled slowly over the concrete bridge separating Tennessee from Georgia state and continued south down Old Highway 2.

From all parts of the camp, people flocked out onto the road as the convoy drove past the Eastwood property to greet old friends. One of them was Emma, high-fiving Colleen when the Murphys' silver Nissan drove by. With the honking of horns and friendly waves, the convoy continued toward the Jonson farm, where the Bentons would setup their new home.

Unlike at their previous camp, there was no existing accommodation at the new site, and the Bentons arrived in a combination of travel trailers, motorhomes, and campervans. Some had previously been Mason's, while others belonged to the original Knoxville group that had first settled at Wasson Lodge.

The Eastwoods were delighted when they saw what was unloaded from the trucks; boxes upon boxes of equipment including compressors, generators, and a whole range of power tools. Being a camp of over thirty men and women, the Bentons had accumulated far more gear than the newly-formed Eastwoods.

Later that afternoon, on one of its last runs, the eight-wheeler truck pulled into the farm with a two-ton Bobcat on board. Getting out the truck's passenger door, a thickset man with sandy hair climbed up onto the flatbed and into the excavator's cabin. A moment later, the Bobcat's diesel engine coughed to life.

Standing close by were Billy and Marcie. Billy nudged Marcie excitedly. "That's exactly what we need to build our pond. You think we'll be able to use it?"

"Absolutely," Marcie replied. As part of the agreement between the two camps, equipment such as this could be made available on request.

The Bobcat moved slowly along its tracks toward the end of the flatbed. "Aren't they going to fix some steel tracks for that thing to drive down?" Marcie asked, frowning as the Bobcat continued to inch forward.

"Doesn't look like it," Billy replied, a puzzled look on his face.

When it reached the edge, the driver stopped, then lowered the boom so that the steel bucket extended down to the ground. Then the Bobcat moved forward again.

"What in tarnation is he doing?" Marcie muttered.

She and Billy watched in amazement as the Bobcat simply drove over the edge until just a small section remained on the flatbed. The bucket, planted firmly on the ground, prevented it from falling over. Working the pilot controls, the driver retracted the bucket and allowed gravity to slowly tilt the Bobcat over until its front tracks tipped to the ground. Then it stopped, leaning over at a precarious thirty-degree angle.

"Now what? That darn thing is stuck halfway between the bed and ground!" Marcie exclaimed.

The bucket lifted and swiveled all the way around until it rested on the flatbed. Expertly managing the controls, the driver drove slowly forward, constantly adjusting the boom that supported the Bobcat's weight until the vehicle was completely on the ground.

"Well, I'll be damned," Marcie said in amazement.

Around them, the semi-circle of people who stood watching broke out into spontaneous applause. Grinning, the driver cut the engine and hopped out of the cabin.

Billy could barely contain his excitement. He tugged Marcie's sleeve. "We need to get that driver to build our pond. He's amazing!"

CHAPTER 12

Chris and Mark were almost out of supplies. They were down to their last bag of rice and two cans of chili carne. They were also running low on coffee, sugar, and cooking oil.

"We need to make a run to Ocoee Town and break into a house," Mark told Chris after a breakfast of sardines and crackers. "That's what I did last time. The stores are all cleaned out."

Like Chris, Mark's head was now completely shaved, other than for the bleached strip that ran down the middle of his scalp. He was bare-chested too, and wore only khaki shorts. Over the past few days, both his and Chris's torsos had become deeply tanned. Unlike Chris, however, who walked everywhere barefoot, Mark needed to wear hiking boots. It was too painful for him otherwise.

That Mark had agreed to shave his head had been no surprise to Chris. He was a leader, Mark his loyal servant. He had seen it in Mark's eyes since the moment of his awakening. Besides, the crow had told him so.

"That's not going to solve our other problem," he said.

"What's that?"

Chris pointed at the Sig Sauer P226 in the holster by Mark's waist. "If we run into trouble, one pistol won't be enough to protect us." He stared into the forest. "And there's plenty of fresh game for us to eat here. We just need rifles to hunt it."

Mark looked doubtful. "I suppose we could go to Cleveland or Chattanooga, and check out the gun stores. I'm not sure there'll be anything left now, though."

Chris shook his head "I know a better place to go. It's closer too."

***

Though he had no memory of being there, Lake Ocoee looked familiar to Chris. When the two emerged from the forest, two miles east of Devil's Point, he knew right away he'd been there before.

Standing next to him, Mark pointed toward the headland jutting out behind the west side of the point. "You can't see it from here, but Wasson Lodge is on the other side."

Chris frowned, thinking hard. "I've heard that name before."

"It's our old camp. The Bentons occupy it now." Mark pointed east, to where a series of small camps were dotted along the lake shore. "We need to find someplace less guarded. This way is better."

After surreptitiously checking out several camps, the pair found one that suited their needs. At a forest clearing next to where a tiny creek ran into the bay, they came across a settler community of around fifteen people. Housed in two-man tents pitched in a wide semi-circle, the two counted nine men and six women in total. From the edge of the forest, they spent several hours spying on the settlers, noting that they kept their supplies in the center tent, pitched closest to the fire pit.

The two crept back into the forest. "We'll break in tonight," Chris told Mark once they were out of earshot. "If we approach it from behind, the forest is only thirty feet away."

The pair returned to the camp at 7 p.m., when the settlers were grilling slabs of venison on a wood fire. The smell of cooked meat drifted toward them, reminding them just how good it was to eat fresh meat.

At 10 p.m., the camp bedded down for the night. Two hundred yards away, Chris and Mark cleared a space in the forest and laid a thin plastic sheet on the ground to give them some protection against the bugs. The two lay down on it and grabbed a few hours' sleep.

At 2:45 a.m., Chris, who had barely slept, roused Mark from his sleep. The two crept through the woods until they were directly opposite where the supply tent was pitched.

Peering around a pine tree, Chris noted there was only one man on watch. He sat by the fire pit with his back to them, where no more than a few embers now glowed. He had a holster strapped to his right hip, and a semi-automatic rifle rested against the log on which he sat.

The pair observed him for forty minutes. During that time, the guard took two tours of the camp, walking slowly around the perimeter before coming back to the fire pit and sitting down again.

After he returned the second time, Chris whispered to Mark, "Give me the Sig."

Mark unbuttoned his holster and handed him the weapon. Then the two stepped out from behind the tree line. In low crouches, they crept forward toward the supply tent, keeping a watchful eye on the guard sitting with his back to them.

Thirty seconds later, they'd covered the distance and crouched behind the back of the tent. Mark pulled out his knife and prodded the tip into the tent's nylon fabric until it tore, then cut a vertical tear big enough for his body to squeeze through.

"Grab as much as you can, I'll keep watch," Chris whispered in his ear.

Mark stuck his head in the gap, then wiggled his shoulders through. Chris passed him the empty backpack the two had brought with them, then peered around the side of the tent and kept watch on the guard. Inside the tent, he could hear Mark rummaging around, though not loud enough for the guard to hear, nor to waken anybody in either of the adjacent tents.

A few minutes later, Mark passed the now bulging pack out to Chris. Soon, he too was outside the tent again.

Chris pointed toward the forest. "Go. I'll meet you back at the camp."

Mark nodded. "Be careful," he whispered. He slung the pack onto his shoulders and scurried back to the edge of the forest. A moment later, he disappeared behind the tree line.

Chris had to wait awhile before the guard finally stood up and made his rounds again. Shortly, he heard boots trudging softly through the grass as the man patrolled the back of the tents. Though he passed only a few feet away from him, he didn't spot Chris, who'd climbed into the supply tent and was holding the torn fabric together with his hands.

As soon as he passed by, Chris climbed out of the tent again. Pistol in hand, he loped up behind the man, his bare feet barely making a sound in the grass. When he got close enough, he snaked his arm around the guard's neck and jerked him back.

The man instinctively let out a cry. Chris rammed the Sig's muzzle up against his cheekbone. "Shut up!" he hissed. "Or you're a dead man."

It was too late. Someone had already heard the guard yell out. From around the camp there came the sound of voices, then someone called out. "Johnny! Where are you?"

Chris dragged Johnny to the ground, then rolled him over so that he lay face first in the grass. He reached across to the man's right side and tore out the pistol from his holster. Sticking it in his pocket, he pulled the rifle off his shoulder.

He stared over at the camp. By now, beams from several flashlights shone around the camp. Keeping his pistol trained on Johnny, he crept backward a few feet, then turned around and sprinted toward the forest.

Behind him, Johnny let out a yell. "Guys! Over here! Sonofabitch stole my rifle!"

"There…I see him!" another voice shouted out.

A moment later, sporadic gunfire broke out. Chris sprinted even faster until he reached the tree line and into cover. Without stopping, he weaved in and out of the trees, letting out a series of victorious whoops as he ran. The tribe's first raid had been a success.

**

It took Mark nearly an hour to make it back to camp. With only a flashlight to guide him, it had been hard navigating in the dark. When he arrived, he shrugged the heavy pack off his shoulders and set it down to one side of the tent. Sweating heavily, he sat cross-legged on the tarpaulin sheet outside and took a long slug of water from his bottle.

While he waited for Chris to return, he thought about how much the man had changed since his injury. Notwithstanding how his eyes would glaze over when he had one of his visions, he'd become more serious too. Since his "awakening," as the two chose to call it, Mark hadn't seen him smile once.

Nonetheless, he believed in the man as much now as he had before. Chris's fierceness and determination hadn't diminished, and it had been those qualities that had led Mark to join his group in the first place. Alone and desperate, he'd been grateful to find someone like Chris to follow. Then the lodge had been attacked and Chris almost killed. It had turned Mark's world upside down again. For those eight days, he'd clung to the hope that Chris might awaken from his coma, because it was the only hope he had.

Now Chris was back, and Mark's world held purpose again. Chris told him of plans to build a tribe more powerful than all the gangs in the Cohutta combined. Mark believed him. The world had been turned on its head, and there was nothing to stop a strong leader rising all the way to the top. In that sense, the new Chris was more fitting than the old one. Things had turned ugly. If they were going to survive, they needed to turn ugly too. Mark smiled to himself. The Mohawks certainly helped with that.

His reverie was broken by the sound of rustling in the bushes. A moment later, Chris strode into the camp. When he got closer, Mark spotted a semi-automatic rifle slung across his shoulder.

"You got the rifle. Cool!"

Chris took it off and examined it. "Daniel Defense MK12," he said, reading the manufacturer details stamped on the metal stock. "An AR-15 of some description, a good one too." He leaned it up against a nearby tree, then handed Mark back his P226. From his pocket, he took out another pistol and showed it to Mark.

Mark handled the weapon. It had a stainless steel barrel and a black grip. "Ruger SR9c," he said, examining it. "Awesome!" He gave it back to Chris, then headed over to the tent and returned with the backpack. "Let's see what we got. I haven't looked yet."

He tipped out the contents of the pack and shone his flashlight over them. Spread across the ground were several packets of spaghetti, three bags of rice, several tins of ham and tuna, a large jar of instant coffee, as well as sugar, salt, and cooking oil.

Mark stared down at the pile with satisfaction. "That should keep us going a while."

"We need more," Chris told him. "Many of those who join us will come unprepared. We need to be ready for them."

"When will they come?" Mark asked, anxious that the tribe begin to grow soon. It had been five days since Chris's awakening, and the tribe still only consisted of the two of them.

"Soon," Chris replied. "Once we've moved to Dream Valley."

Mark stared at him in confusion. "Dream Valley? Where is that?"

"Somewhere close by. I just need to find it."

CHAPTER 13

Two days after the arrival of the Bentons, "Billy's Pond Project" officially got underway.

The location had already been selected. Billy and Marcie had chosen a large hollow at the bottom of a sloping meadow at the southeast corner of the farm, where the land became uneven and stretched up into the hills. A small creek ran close by that would make the pond easy to fill when the time came.

Walter had yet to inspect the site. That morning, Billy brought him over to it across the rough, hilly ground. As they came down an overgrown footpath into the hollow, Marcie, who had been waiting for them, stared at Walter when the two arrived. "What's that for?" she asked, pointing to the shovel he carried in one hand.

"To check the soil," Walter replied, panting slightly. "Seeing as you don't intend putting down pond liner, we need to make sure the area you've chosen is suitable for holding water." He surveyed the designated area, a tangled mess of thick brush, weeds, and saplings. "Seems like a good spot. Only a couple of big trees to cut down." He pointed higher up the hill. "I plan on building my waterwheel up at the creek. It won't have any effect on your pond, though."

After thirty minutes of testing, Walter gave the site the thumbs up. The soil had an adequate mix of clay and loam, both fine soils with low permeability. Without it, the proposed basin quite literally wouldn't hold water.

With a well-practiced stride, Walter measured the perimeter. He "stepped off" the distance, each step equal to two and a half feet. "This is how people measured land in the old days," he told Billy, who was walking alongside him. "Far easier than using a measuring tape."

The saucer-shaped basin measured roughly four hundred by three hundred and fifty feet. Walter did a quick mental calculation. "That's a little over three acres. Plenty of room for stocking fish."

"Why did you calculate it in acres?" Billy asked.

"It's how you measure the surface area of water," Walter explained. "It'll come in useful when calculating the various ratios of fish to stock. They're normally calculated by the acre. All right, I'll head over and talk to Ned, see if he'll lend us his excavator for a few days." He frowned. "Been a while since I've used one. I'm sure I'll get the hang of it soon enough."

Marcie hesitated a moment before speaking. "Nothing personal, Walter, but Billy and I already have someone in mind for that. We were hoping you might persuade him to help us."

***

Early the following morning, Rob Pollard, the Benton man who'd maneuvered the Bobcat off the flatbed, arrived at the site. Walter had talked to him in person the previous evening, and persuaded him to build the pond, explaining that a twelve-year-old boy named Billy was most anxious for him to do the work.

Prior to the pandemic, Pollard had been in construction, which was where he'd gotten his experience operating plant machinery, and he'd been the one to build the defensive trenches back at the old Benton camp.

Standing on the Bobcat's foot rail, Walter guided him around the south side of the farm, then up and down the hill leading to the pond site, where Billy and Marcie were waiting. They could hear the Bobcat clanking noisily on its tracks long before it came into view.

When he reached them, Pollard cut the engine and got out of the cabin. Walter hopped down off the rail and walked over to them. "Rob, this is Marcie and Billy," Walter said, introducing everybody.

"We saw you unload the excavator the other day," Billy said as the two shook hands. He looked up at the Benton man. "You know any other tricks?"

Pollard laughed. "I'll see if I can think of something," he said in a laconic drawl, then put his hand on Billy's shoulder. "Later on, I'll give you a lesson on how to operate the excavator. How does that sound?"

Billy's eyes shone with excitement. "Cool! I'd love that!"

Pollard looked across to where Marcie and Billy had marked out the circumference of the proposed pond, using sticks with colored rags attached to them to make them easily visible. "Now let's take a look at this site, see if I can't figure out what to do."

Ten minutes later, he came back from surveying the area. "Looks straightforward enough," he said.

"How long do you think it'll take to build?" Walter asked.

"About three days ought to do it," Pollard replied. "Half a day of clearing, two solid days digging." With that, he walked back to the Bobcat and got to work.

He hauled out some equipment from the back of the machine. One of the items was a chainsaw, which he used to cut down the trees, saplings, and the larger of the shrubs. Watching from close by, Billy instructed him not to cut the tree stumps too low, as they would provide habitat for the fish.

Once he was done, Pollard climbed into the Bobcat and used the pincer attached to the bucket to pick up the saplings and dump them on the far side of the perimeter. The two trees were too big for that, and he had to attach chains to them and drag them away. Later, they would be chopped up for firewood. After that, he used the Bobcat's bucket to clear the brush.

The whole time, Billy stood close by, watching intently. Both Walter and Marcie had left, Walter to work on his hydro project, Marcie to supervise work in the field.

Just as he'd estimated, it took Pollard the entire morning to clear the site. Shortly after 1 p.m., several neat piles of trees, shrubs, and brush were ready for chopping or burning. Pollard cut the Bobcat's engine and headed over to the Benton camp to take his lunch.

Billy surveyed the area with satisfaction. The two tree trunks had been cut to a height of six feet and remained as structures for the fish, and a few large boulders and some old logs had been left as well.

After lunch, Pollard returned and began with the digging. He climbed into the excavator's cabin, put on his seatbelt, and started the engine. Releasing the lock lever, he pushed the two travel sticks forward, and the vehicle trundled forward on its tracks. Once in position, he lowered the boom, curled the bucket to scoop out a large mound of earth, and dumped it behind the pond's marked boundary.

"We have to make some artificial structures," Billy told Marcie and Walter, who'd returned after lunch to check on progress. "Fish need plenty of good habitat, either to get away from predators or to spawn."

Marcie nodded. "Animals like structures. Put a dozen cows in a ten-acre field with just one tree in the middle, pretty soon all twelve of those cows will be standing under it."

"In the shallow waters, we'll need to build hiding places for bait fish," Billy continued. "Also, some areas for plankton and algae to grow. In the deeper waters, predators need to have places to wait in ambush too."

Walter stared down at Billy appreciatively. "You've become quite an expert, haven't you? Tell you what, why don't you come over to my workshop? Let's start making some of those structures now. They can't be that difficult to make."

It turned out there was quite a science to building fish structures. While some were straightforward enough, no more than a few hollow blocks cemented together, others, such as honey hole shrubs with their flexible snag-free limbs, took a little more ingenuity. Walter found some pieces of PVC pipe and polythene strips to build those. Standing beside him, Billy QA-ed each final product, making sure there were no sharp edges where the fish might cut themselves.

By the end of the day, the two had made several prototypes. "We need to build a lot more," Billy told Walter as he bolted the workshop door and locked it with a heavy-duty padlock. "A good habitat needs at least a dozen structures per acre."

"Really?" Walter said in alarm. He hadn't planned on spending the whole of the next day building fish habitats—he had a waterwheel to build. He thought for a moment. "You know what? There's someone at Camp Benton with a keen interest in fishing. This is right up his alley. How about I introduce the two of you?"

Billy nodded. "That'd be cool."

A smile played on Walter's lips. "I have to warn you, though, he's a little excitable. A little hard to understand too. All the same, I'll introduce you to him."

CHAPTER 14

The next morning, Walter strolled over to the Benton camp to seek out Jonah Murphy. Over the past few days, the camp had been a hive of activity, and the sounds of drills, hammers, and saws could be heard all day long. Walter marveled at how quickly things were taking shape. The cooking, washing, and shower facilities had been dismantled from the old YMCA camp and already re-installed at the new site. So had many of the cabins, which people had chosen to relocate rather than live in trailers. Even the dining hall had been hauled up and reassembled. It had been the focal point for the Benton community and they were delighted to see it rebuilt.

It was there that Walter found Jonah taking his breakfast. Winding around the clutter of tables, he made his way over to where Jonah sat with Colleen and Monica. Walter had gotten to know the two women reasonably well from their time at the Eastwood camp, and both greeted him with friendly smiles.

He sat down opposite Jonah, who looked at him inquiringly. Walter hadn't seen him since the day of Mason's defeat.

He got straight down to business. "I don't know whether you've heard or not, but a few of my people are building a freshwater aquaculture system. A young man by the name of Billy is in charge. Actually, he's real young. Twelve years old, to be exact, but he's got a head on his shoulders of a forty-year-old man."

Jonah stared at him, confused. "Sounds like a great chap. What's that got to do with me, though?"

Walter went on to explain the exact nature of the project. Soon, Jonah was listening avidly. While he had never come across the term "freshwater aquaculture system" before, the word "fish" cropped up often enough to catch his attention. By the time Walter got to explaining how the project required somebody with good fishing knowledge to help stock the pond, the Irishman was practically frothing at the mouth.

"If it's fishing know-how yer looking for, there's no better man than me to give yis a dig out," he said excitedly. "I've caught more fish in me life than most people have had hot dinners."

"That's why you were the first name that popped into my head. By the way, we're building some artificial structures for the pond today," Walter added casually. "I don't suppose you want to give us a *dig out* with that too? It'll give you a chance to get to know Billy."

Jonah's eyes lit up like pinballs. "Pond structures? For the fish, yeh say? I'm game ball for that!"

"Excellent." Walter checked his watch. It was 8:40 a.m., and he'd told Billy he would be at the workshop by 8:30. He stared at Jonah's empty plate. "Well, if you've no other plans, how about we get started on it now?"

"Sound as a bell." Jonah rose from his seat and looked across the table. "You were right, Monica. I'm liking this Alli-coosey Valley more and more. Now, ladies, I have to love yis and leave yis. I'm off to meet Billy the Kid. We're about to have a serious natter about all things fish."

"Do that, Jonah," his wife replied. "Us ladies will get on just fine without you."

Bidding Colleen and Monica good day, Walter followed Jonah out of the dining hall, chuckling to himself.

Mission accomplished. He'd found somebody else to help build Billy's fish structures. He just hoped the two got along. Their personalities were like chalk and cheese.

To his relief, Jonah and Billy got along just fine. Arriving at his workshop, he found the young boy waiting for him, anxious to get on with the work.

"Billy, this is Jonah, the man I was telling you about last night. When I told him about your project, he absolutely begged me to be allowed on board. That right, Jonah?"

"Keen as mustard," Jonah said. He extended his arm and shook Billy's hand vigorously. "So, you're the little genius who's building this...aqua...aquagarial pond system?"

Billy nodded. "It's an aquaculture freshwater ecosystem."

"But it involves fish, right?" Jonah winked at Walter. "Yeh didn't bring me out here on a wild catfish chase, did yeh?"

Walter chuckled. "Oh, it involves fish all right." He unlocked the workshop door and slid it open on its railer. "Come on in. I'll show you the prototype structures we made yesterday."

Walter showed Jonah around the workshop, pointing out where all the tools were kept. Jonah admired the selection. "Y'ev a fine bunch of tools here. I'm pretty handy at the old carpentry meself, if yeh ever need a hand. I just rebuilt me and Colleen's cabin we lived in down at the lake. She didn't fancy living in a trailer."

"I'll make a note of that," Walter told him. "Just so happens I'm starting on a carpentry project soon."

He took Jonah and Billy over to one of the workbenches. "Why don't you two get started? If you need me, I'll be working on my own project," he said, pointing over at the second workbench at the far side of the barn. "Billy, grill Jonah. Make sure he knows what he's talking about."

Over the course of the next few hours while they built several honey hole shrubs, each a slightly different shape and design, Billy quizzed Jonah on his knowledge of fish. He quickly became satisfied with the Irishman's breadth and knowledge. While Jonah's main expertise was in how to catch them, he knew plenty about how to stock and farm them too. Ireland had many trout farms, and Jonah had visited a few in his time.

Soon the two were discussing the finer points on what varieties they should stock, and in what ratios. There was a science to the matter that both appreciated. One couldn't just throw a bunch of fish into a pond and expect them to thrive. Minnows and other bait fish needed to be stocked, and the ratios and sizes of predatory fish taken into account too.

"Yeh need to establish yer food chain just right," Jonah told Billy. "Especially if you're stocking bass." He grinned. "They don't call them bigmouths for nothing. If there's not enough forage, they'll gobble everything up in sight. Pretty soon yeh'll have nothing in yer pond but muck and weeds. We should stock catfish and bream as well. There's plenty of them here in the Conassauga."

Billy nodded. "Sure, but I want trout in the pond too."

Jonah looked doubtful. "Trout need cold, clean water. Without moving water, the pond needs to be deep. Especially in summertime."

"Most of it will be about eight foot deep, though there'll be some parts that are deeper. Will that be okay?"

Jonah thought for a moment. "We might chuck in a few brownies. See how they get on."

"Why brownies?"

"Brown trout can survive in warmer water. They don't mind it murky either."

"My pond is not going to be murky," Billy said firmly.

"Stagnant water always gets murky. There's not much that can be done about that."

Billy digested this. "I hope the brownies like it. I really want trout in the pond."

"Don't worry, we'll figure it out," Jonah reassured him. "Back in Ireland, they didn't call me the 'trout whisperer' for nothing."

Over at his workbench, Walter practically doubled-up. The Irishman was a hoot. The "trout whisperer," now that was a first. Despite his initial reservations over whether the two would get on, it appeared that Jonah's personality and infectious humor had won the more reserved Billy over. In life, opposites often attract. This was most definitely a case in point.

At 12:30 p.m., the three broke for lunch, comprised of freshly baked cornbread and cold cuts of venison that Greta brought over for them. The thickly sliced bread was delicious. Hot out of the oven, Greta had drizzled olive oil over them, and the venison was served with cranberry sauce on the side. In the coming months, delicacies such as these would inevitably get used up, and everybody appreciated them while they lasted.

Afterward, Walter returned to his workbench and continued with the design for his waterwheel. The ratios between the driving pulley and sprockets that would turn the alternator needed to be calibrated just right. Too fast and it would burn out, too slow and the wheel wouldn't generate enough power. The properties of the materials he intended using were important too. The wood would only support so much weight, and while the steel parts of the frame would support more, they needed a firmer mounting.

Thankfully, he had taken two reference books with him from Knoxville: *Ugly's Electrical References Guide* and *Pocket Ref*. While *Ugly's* pertained to all things electrical, he used *Pocket Ref* for everything else, and both well-thumbed copies were put to good use.

He would need to design the permanent magnet alternator as well. Technically, this would be the most difficult part of the project. The modification to the Camry's alternator involved rebuilding its stator and rotor entirely, then configuring the rare-earth magnets precisely. While he'd read up on such things before, this would be the first time he would actually build one, and it would require all his engineering skills.

By the end of the day, he was happy with the progress he'd made. At the other workbench, Jonah and Billy were doing well. Over a dozen pond structures had been built, and sat in a neat row along one side of the barn.

The light was dimming from the skies, and Walter's stomach was rumbling. He checked his watch to see it was already after 5 p.m. The day had flown by.

"I don't know about you two, but I'm starving. Let's call it a day, shall we?"

"Another day, another dollar. Isn't that what youse yanks say?" Jonah said, grinning.

"Not anymore. More like, another day, another bullet to barter." Walter clapped him on the back. "Come on, you're eating with us tonight. Beer's on me."

"Lovely jubbly. Just the one, mind. I'm cutting down on the old gargle." Jonah looked skyward. "Orders from above."

"Who do you mean?" Walter asked, confused. "You mean *God?*"

Jonah nodded. "I told the big fella that if he kept Colleen safe while I was stuck at the lake with Mason, I'd cut down on me intake. You know, that I'd be a little more…" He struggled to come up with the right word.

"Moderate?" Walter suggested helpfully as the three left the workshop and he locked up.

"That's it. Everything in moderation, they say. 'Course, nothing too drastic," Jonah added hastily. "It's not like I can't enjoy meself every once in awhile. And if yeh don't tell Colleen how many I have, that'd be even better."

Walter smiled. "I wouldn't dream of it," he told the Irishman. "As to God, I can't help you there. You might have some explaining to do."

CHAPTER 15

Chris had regained the weight he'd lost since his injury, or so Mark told him. He himself had no memory of that. He felt good, though, and his morning exercise routine helped bring his body back to peak shape.

His mind was another matter. The crow continued to appear regularly on his shoulder, whispering things to him through the hole in his head. It presented him with startling images, told him the things he needed to accomplish, and urged him never to forget the destiny that lay before him.

In calmer moments, he recognized that the crow had something to do with his injury. A bullet sat lodged deep within his brain tissue, leaving a trail of broken neurological wiring in its wake. Still, he liked his mind just as it was. The crow's visions showed him the path to his destiny, and he hoped it would never leave.

***

Chris and Mark continued their raids along Lake Ocoee's southern shore. Their MO remained the same. During the day, they would patiently observe where the settlers stowed their supplies, then, deep in the night, they would steal into the camps and take them. As well as food, they pilfered medicine, gas cylinders, flashlights, batteries, razors, saws, hammers, axes, ammunition, and a whole range of other items.

On one of their raids, Chris took down another guard. Now Mark too had a semi-automatic rifle, a US-made AK-47 variant. On another raid, the two stole a large tan-colored canvas tarpaulin. Unused and still folded up in its packaging, it measured eighteen by thirty feet and weighted over fifty pounds. "This will be my home when we move to Dream Valley," Chris informed Mark.

What was harder to come by were hunting rifles. Settlers kept their weapons inside their tents, which were too dangerous to break into. Chris soon came up with a solution to obtain these too.

Whenever a group left to go hunting, he and Mark would follow them and wait for the opportunity to waylay the first person who strayed off on their own. In this manner, the pair collected: a Marlin .22 rifle, excellent for hunting small game such as squirrel and rabbits; a Mossberg 12-gauge pump-action shotgun for shooting birds such as quail, woodcock, and grouse; and two larger caliber rifles to bring down deer and feral pig—an Anschuz 1781 chambered in .30/06, and a Browning chambered in .243 Win.

There was always a look of astonishment on a settler's face when they saw the bare-chested men with shaved heads and bleached Mohawks step out menacingly from behind the trees. Once relieved of their rifle, pistol, buck knife, and any other valuables they carried, the pair would run back into the forest letting out maniacal whoops and yells, and it didn't take long before they overheard themselves being referred to as "the scourge of the forest" by the irate lakeside settlers.

As well as food and weapons, Chris also liked to steal books. Most who arrived at the Cohutta had little hunting or survival experience, and many brought books with them to help learn these skills. Once they got their hands on one, Chris and Mark would spend hours reading it, then head into the forest to practice the new techniques they'd learned.

Soon, not only did their hunting and fishing skills improve, but they became adept at trapping, and small game such as rabbit, squirrel, and possum quickly appeared on the menu.

On one occasion, the two confronted a settler with a crossbow. There was a look of satisfaction on Chris's face as he relieved the man of his possession. Mark grinned delightedly. "Awesome. Just what the tribe needs!"

The crossbow was a Predator model. It came with a high-quality scope, and a set of twenty two-foot-long arrows. Chris spent hours practicing with it, and once he'd learned the proper hold, most of his rifle skills easily transferred over.

Each morning, he and Mark would head deep into the forest's interior. They became adept at recognizing game trails, patiently tracking their prey through the trees until they got into a good shooting position. Chris was the better hunter. He would stalk a buck or a wild boar until he got within thirty yards of it, uncock his bow, take aim, and bring the animal down.

Some days, they made a hide close to a game trail, and simply waited for their prey to come to them. That style of hunting quickly bored Chris. They were warriors, and warriors hunted; they didn't just wait for their prey to walk up to them.

On one of their hunting trips, the two ventured into an area they'd never been to before, where a series of verdant hills covered in old forest growth dominated the vista. They hiked up the nearest one along a trail, bright sunshine filtering through the leaves of the hickory and oak trees.

Reaching the ridge line, they gazed down into an isolated valley below. It was lightly wooded with copses of fir, spruce, and mountain laurel, and at the bottom, a fast-flowing river passed through it.

Chris froze in his tracks, staring down at it.

"What's up?" Mark asked him.

"This is it. This is where we set up our new camp."

***

Dream Valley was a fifty-minute hike from their current camp. The two had accumulated a lot of gear, and it took them until the following morning to transfer it all.

On a shallow slope fifty yards from the river was a natural clearing surrounded by sparse woodland. It was the location Chris had seen in his dreams. Mark looked at him uncertainly when he told him. "Sure," he said after a few seconds. "Awesome."

The two set about building a shelter using the recently stolen tarp. They created a simple, flat-topped tent by running two parallel lengths of paracord ten feet apart, and attached the ends to the sturdiest branches among the trees. One of the lines was attached to its anchor points slightly lower than the other, to allow runoff when it rained. Once both cords had been properly secured, they draped the canvas over them and secured the tarpaulin to the ground with tent stakes.

Chris stepped back and stared at his new home with satisfaction. Eighteen feet long, ten feet wide, and with a high ceiling, it was far roomier than the small two-man tent the two had been sleeping in until now. Set among the trees, with its tan roof, it was well camouflaged from anyone looking down from the ridge.

"That'll do for now," said Chris. "Come wintertime, we'll need to insulate the floor. For the moment, you can stay with me."

"For the moment?" Mark echoed.

"A chief needs a woman to share his bed with," Chris told him. "Once I've found one, you'll need to move."

The two spent the rest of the day organizing the camp. After storing their valuables in the tent, they built a fire pit at the center of the clearing, then Mark cut down several branches and built a cone-shaped hut to serve as their larder, tacking a plastic sheet around it to protect it from the rain. In it, he stored their two plastic food lockers, their pots and pans, and cooking utensils. Outside, he placed the gas stove and a five-gallon water container.

That evening, the two sat by the fire pit eating venison haunches they had roasted over the grill.

"You say you will have a woman soon…" Mark ventured after they'd eaten. "How about me? Will I have one too?"

"Once I have chosen mine, you shall have whoever you choose," Chris replied. "You saved my life. That deserves a reward."

"But when will they arrive?" Mark persisted. "It's been over a week now since your awakening."

Chris stared at him "You doubt my vision of what is to come?"

"Of course not! I-I just want to know when, that's all."

Chris echoed the words that the crow told him that morning. "Soon a storm will come to the valley. When it passes, we shall find the first of our people."

Mark looked at him excitedly. "Awesome!"

CHAPTER 16

The following day, Walter showed up at the workshop at 8:30 a.m., where he found Jonah and Billy already waiting for him.

"That's what I like to see," he told the two as he unlocked the door. "Enthusiasm for the job at hand."

"Robby's almost finished the pond, so we need to get cracking," Jonah replied. "We were just about to pick that lock of yours when yeh showed up, weren't we, Billy?"

"No we weren't!" Billy exclaimed in shock. Jonah nudged him in the ribs. "Uh...yeah. A minute longer and we would have."

Walter laughed. "I think you're starting to get the hang of Jonah's humor." He slid open the door and let the two in. "The trick is to understand what he's saying first."

He quickly gathered some tools and headed out again, leaving the two to finish work on the pond structures.

"Hey, where yeh going?" Jonah shouted after him.

"To see a man about a dog. Isn't that what they say in your neck of the woods?" Walter called out over his shoulder.

He made his way across to the southeast corner of the property and hiked up the hill. At the top, he gazed over the far side and into the hollow, pleased to see the progress that had been made. Like Jonah said, the pond was almost ready.

Shaped like a soup plate, it had areas that would provide both deep and shallow waters. The deeper areas could be used by fish to retreat to during wintertime, while in the shallower zones, pea gravel had been deposited to encourage many varieties to reproduce. Perhaps the trout would thrive here after all, Walter thought to himself with a smile.

He climbed higher into the hills and headed up to the section of the creek where he planned to install his waterwheel, a spot where the gradient dropped steeply for about thirty feet. Behind it, the land flattened out and the water naturally collected in a shallow pool.

Using the shovel he'd brought with him, he constructed a simple dam with local rocks and boulders, leaving a one-foot gap for the water to continue on downstream. By the time he'd finished, the pool had grown larger, spreading slowly across its shallow banks to form a semi-circular lagoon-shaped area.

He tested the water flow over the drop. "That's what I'm talking about," he said with a satisfied grunt. For the waterwheel to generate electricity, it would require a minimum of three feet of fall, and twenty gallons per minute of flow. His newly-constructed dam provided plenty more than that.

He took several measurements to determine the length of the spillway he needed to build, making detailed sketches in his notebook. The spillway would capture the water tumbling over the drop and channel it into the buckets of the waterwheel.

Once he was satisfied, he set off down the hill again. On the way back to the workshop, he thought about what Jonah told him the previous day when he'd professed to being "pretty handy" at carpentry. Though building the waterwheel wasn't overly complicated, it required someone with good carpentry skills. With Ned Granger's permission, Walter was confident he could rope the amiable Irishman into helping him with his project.

***

Late that afternoon, Pollard completed construction on the pond. Wearing gumboots, Walter, Jonah, and Billy walked down into the muddy hollow and inspected the work.

Pollard had done his job perfectly. The pond conformed to the exact design Billy had shown him in his book. Walter was pleased with the engineering aspects as well. The bottom of the huge basin had been agitated with the end of the excavator's shovel so that the fine soil had sunk to the ground, then compacted to hold water. The pond's banks, formed from the excavated soil, had been mixed with rocks and root stocks to strengthen it, then run over with the Bobcat, compacting it.

Lodged against the banks, several large boulders had been positioned so that they would protrude out of the water. The boulders would accumulate heat from the sun and raise the water's temperature. In winter, this would help prevent the pond from freezing over, decreasing the potential risk of oxygen deficiency.

Pollard had also installed an overflow pipe so that, during bad weather, it would take out excess rain and runoff water. He told Billy that he would need to fit a wire mesh over it so that the fish couldn't swim out.

"You've done this before, haven't you?" Walter said, staring over to where Pollard sat on top of the bank smoking a cigarette.

The Benton man grinned. "More times than I can remember." After all three thanked him, he climbed into the Bobcat and drove back to Camp Benton.

"Come on!" Jonah said, rubbing his hands gleefully. "Let's chuck in these pond structures and fill this baby up!"

The structures had been hauled up to the site earlier by Jonah and Billy. The three carried them down into the basin, and under Billy's supervision, began placing them around the pond. Every now and then Jonah made a suggestion as to where one might be better installed. With his years of fishing experience, he knew precisely the types of habitats different species preferred to dwell in.

The final measure was to spread fertilizer on the bottom of the pond to provide some initial food for the fish. The previous day, Jonah had spotted the bags in one of the barns and made the suggestion. The twenty-five-kilo bags were too heavy for Billy to manage, and it was left up to Jonah to fetch them while Walter went off and got the water pump.

"This'll fatten up the stock nicely," Jonah told Billy, sweating as he tipped the last bag of fertilizer over the basin's floor.

A short time later, Walter appeared at the top of the hill pushing an old rusting wheelbarrow containing his water pump. Pausing for breath, he continued higher into the hills.

When he reached the creek, he lifted out the pump and placed it on the riverbank. He took out a long length of hose he'd brought with him, attached one end to the pump's outlet, then unwound the hose as he walked down the hill, placing the other end in the pond.

Back up at the creek, he dropped the three-inch-thick intake hose that came with the pump into the stream. "All right," he said, sweating heavily. "Let's see how much water this sucker can shift."

He started the seven-horsepower motor, and the pump began to noisily suck water out of the creek. Moments later, water came gushing out the far end and into the basin.

"How long will it take to fill?" Billy asked Walter excitedly when he came down and joined him.

"According to the manual, the motor pumps thirteen thousand gallons of water an hour. Let's see, one inch of water over one acre is 27,000 gallons…multiplied by three acres at an average of, say, eight feet of depth, equals…*hmmm*…one hell of a long time."

Billy's face dropped. "Not today?"

Walter shook his head. "Not today. In fact I'll have to refill the gas tank at least once. We'll know in the morning whether our pond holds water or not. Don't worry," he added, seeing Billy's anxious look. "Rob did a fantastic job. I'm sure it'll be fine."

***

When Walter arrived at the workshop the next morning, there was no sign of Billy or Jonah. He headed up to the pond and found the two sitting on the bank.

After greeting them, he checked the water level. It was two inches below the overflow pipe. "Not bad," he said. "When I came here last night, the water had already reached the pipe and was flowing back out again."

Jonah nodded. "I guessed you'd been here. The pump was off, but there's still gas in the tank."

Billy frowned. "But if the level has dropped since last night, doesn't that mean the pond is leaking?"

Walter squatted beside him and peered into the pond. "I think it's okay. You got to expect some subsidence after all that digging. If the pond was leaking, most of the water would have drained by now." He stood up again. "Well, that's phase one complete. Now all we got to do is stock it with fish."

"I want to put forage fish in first," Billy said. "They're bottom of the food chain. But we need traps for that, and a good place to set them."

"I know a certain person who will know all about that." Walter glanced at Billy. "Maybe it's time for Jonah to be introduced to Mr. Hillbilly. What do you think?"

"Great idea, Walter!" Billy exclaimed. "Clete's bound to know where to find some traps."

Jonah chuckled. "Mr. Hillbilly? Sounds just the kind of geezer I need to meet."

CHAPTER 17

Walter found Clete outside his trailer, where he was cleaning his hunting rifle, a Nosler M48 Liberty. With its walnut stock and match-grade, hand-lapped barrels, he suspected Clete hadn't owned it before the pandemic. The top of the range weapon came with a retail sticker of around two thousand dollars.

After a brief chat, Walter took him over to the farmhouse where Jonah and Billy were waiting in the kitchen.

Jonah and Clete had never been formally introduced until now, and it took a few minutes for the two men to size each other up. Both asked a few probing questions before quickly realizing that they had a lot in common, namely, a cheerful disposition, a love of fishing, and a certain fondness for a drink or two. Soon, they were gabbing away like they'd known each other for years. A short time later, Walter slipped out the back door and headed back to his workshop to continue with the design of his waterwheel.

He left Billy with the two men. Direct as ever, the young boy soon turned the conversation in the direction he required. "Clete, Walter says you know where we can get traps for catching baitfish. We need them to stock the pond."

"Minnow traps? So happens I got a few in my trailer," Clete replied in his customary chirpy voice. "Saw them up in

Walmart awhile back, thought they might come in useful." He stood up from the table. "Hang on there and I'll show you them."

As he left the room, Jonah rubbed his hands delightedly. "Now there's a handy fella to know." He ruffled Billy's hair. "We'll have this pond of yours stocked in no time at all."

"Can I go out with you to set the traps?" Billy asked. "I want to see how it's done."

"Sure," Jonah replied. "So long as Walter gives you permission to leave the camp."

Clete returned shortly with three minnow traps. Made out of a heavy-duty vinyl-dipped mesh, they were torpedo-shaped with a cone entrance on either side, designed so that the minnows would swim along the funnel, through the narrow end, and into the main cage where they would become trapped. Sturdily built, they were easy to pull apart, insert the bait, and clip back together again.

"Perfect for catching two-inchers," Jonah said, inspecting one of the traps. "What will we use for bait? Back in Ireland, I used pieces of white bread, but seeing as the only sliced pan left must be green with mold by now, we'll need to use something else."

"I got a stash of cat food. That works pretty good too," Clete told him. "This is a good time of year to catch fatheads. There'll be plenty of red horse and shad too. They spawn continually during the summer months. Maybe you'll catch some shiners as well."

"What are they?" Billy asked.

"They're super-fast minnows that bass find harder to catch," Jonah told him. "They only spawn once a year, though, so they're difficult to find."

"I know where to go," Clete said confidently. "There's a spot not too far from here that's perfect for catching them. We can go there now, if you want."

Jonah glanced at Billy. "Let me check with Walter and make sure it's okay to bring the young fella with us, then we're good to go."

Twenty minutes later, the three drove out of camp in Clete's F-150. Sitting in the back of the truck were two Benton men who Jonah had rounded up, both armed with semi-automatic rifles. Walter had informed him that it was fine for Billy to go with them so long as they took a security detail.

They drove northwest along Sheeds Creek Road, following the Conassauga River for a few miles before turning off onto a smaller road and heading east. For another twenty minutes, Clete guided the Ford down a network of country roads, then turned up a dirt and gravel road. On either side, the brush grew high and wild, thumping loudly against the Ford's fender as he tore up the track.

After a couple of miles, they turned a bend and a river that ran parallel to the road came into view. Wide and slow moving, it was perfect for catching minnows.

Clete pulled up along the riverbank. "This is it," he said, cutting the engine.

The three got out and walked around to the back of the truck. In the load bed lay the three traps, which had already been baited. Back at Eastwood, Billy had spooned a generous portion of cat food into three socks so that it wouldn't float away.

"Holy cow, that stinks!" one of the guards said, wrinkling his nose as he handed out the traps.

"Them tiddlers are going to love it," Jonah replied. "If yer lucky, we'll save some for yeh later."

Along with Clete and Billy, he carried a trap over to the riverbank. Clete pointed down at the river's edge, where the water was only a couple of inches high. It was a baking hot day, and dragonflies, water striders, and all sorts of insects hovered over water. "Look Billy, there's a bunch of baby minnows right there swimming around. See them?"

Billy leaned his head over. "I see them. Wow, they're tiny!"

"Yep, looks like they just hatched. Now, pay attention. Watch how I do this." Clete lowered the trap he held in his right hand, the torpedo ends perpendicular to the river. Attached to the handle was a long piece of cord. "The water is deep here, so we don't need to throw them very far. The trick is to face them with one funnel upriver, the other downriver. You don't want the trap sideways, because minnows swim up and down river, not sideways."

He swung out his arm and released the trap. It sailed into the air and landed five feet away with a splash. Immediately, it began to sink. "There she goes. She'll just lie there on the bottom. Now, your turn. See if you can throw your trap past mine."

Billy lowered his arm. He took a couple of tentative swings, outstretched his arm, then released the trap. It flew through the air and hit the water about three feet past Clete's.

"Nice throw!" the Tennessean exclaimed. "You're a natch at this!"

Billy grinned, pleased with himself.

Jonah threw his trap out next. It landed a few feet past Billy's, and quickly disappeared from sight. Stepping back, he tied up his line to the trunk of a sturdy shrub nearby. "We'll haul them up in a few hours," he said. "I'm pretty sure we'll have caught a few pounds between us by then."

He walked back to the pickup, leaned over the tailgate, and pulled out several items: a plastic bucket, three fishing rods, and a canvas bag. There was a clinking sound as he unzipped the bag.

"Beer for the men, lemonade for Billy," he said, handing the guards a beer each, then headed back to the riverbank where Clete was helping Billy secure his line.

"Can I have a beer too?" Billy asked hopefully.

"No yeh can't. Yer only twelve years old," Jonah said sternly, laying the rods out on the ground. He rummaged around the bag and handed the boy a can of 7Up. "That's all yeh'll be drinking until yer eighteen years old, so get used it."

Billy put on a glum face. Clete chuckled as he accepted a beer. "Looks like you got someone strict watching you, Billy. Too bad."

"A boy needs that," Jonah replied firmly. "My old man put manners on me when I was his age, I'll tell yeh that for nothing."

He sat down on the grass bank and twisted off the cap of his beer bottle. Taking a long slug, he pointed fifty yards farther upstream to where a group of large boulders protruded out into the river. "Clete, yeh say there's trout in this stream? That looks a nifty place to cast our rods. Let's see if we can grab ourselves a tasty dinner while we're here."

***

Several beers and two 7Ups later, the three returned to check their traps. Billy walked along the riverbank between the two men, proudly carrying four medium-sized trout on a stringer. That was dinner sorted, as Jonah had put it.

They hauled their traps out of the water and onto the bank. Jonah leaned over and peered into his. Below, on the trap floor, hundreds of fatheads, shad, and red horse minnows flapped around in a panic. Billy and Clete's traps were similarly full, and between them they had several pounds.

Jonah had brought several polythene bags with him. The three lowered one each into the river and filled them with water, after which they emptied the minnows into them. Knotting the tops tightly, they took them over to the pickup and placed them in the truck bed.

"That's a big pond, we'll need to make a few more trips," Jonah said as he opened the truck door and hoisted Billy up onto the seat. "Then it's onto the big fellas, like trout, bass, and catfish. Can't wait for that. How about you, Mr. Hillbilly?"

"If that's your way of inviting me on your next fishing trip, count me in," the Tennessean replied, climbing into the cabin. He looked up at the skies as he started the engine. Over the past hour, it had become increasingly more overcast. "Looks like there's a storm coming. Wouldn't be surprised if it hits us in the next day or so."

He switched on the truck stereo. Below it, an iPhone sat in the divider, cabled up to the stereo's auxiliary input. "How about we listen to a little country music on the way home?"

"*Ooh, yeah*, love me some bluegrass," Jonah said in an atrocious American accent. "What yeh got, dude?"

Clete grinned. "Just the thing to tap your feet to."

He jabbed the play button and for the next thirty minutes, the three hooted and hollered to *Foggy Mountain Breakdown* played at full volume along with a host of other "golden oldies" as Jonah put it. Even the two guards in the back stomped their feet.

In between songs, Jonah leaned back in his seat contentedly. Perhaps this Alli-Couzy Valley, or whatever it was called, wasn't such a bad spot after all.

CHAPTER 18

Sixty-one miles southwest of Bogota, the town of Melgar was known by Colombians as the "City of Swimming Pools." With its mild sub-tropical climate, it was the perfect getaway destination for Bogotanos to escape their cold, high-altitude plateau, and every weekend the town's five thousand pools were put to good use, along with the dozens of nightclubs that served the influx of revelers.

As well as being an inland resort, Melgar was somewhat incongruously also home to Tolemaida Air Base, one of the country's largest military installations. Colombian Special Forces trained there regularly, and as such, there was a constant flow of US "military consultants" and support personnel in and out of the base. Although unofficial, they even had their very own barracks built on the grounds.

Among the US servicemen were several intelligence officers. In war, intelligence played a key role that could determine the success or failure of a mission. In that respect, a drug war wasn't any different, and "intel" provided tactical information about the well-armed drug traffickers and their cocaine laboratories prior to any raid.

One such officer was US Army Lieutenant Max Kohler. Five-nine, slightly-built, with sandy hair and expressionless gray eyes, he'd been stationed in Colombia for over three years and specialized in monitoring the country's paramilitary activities.

The right-wing United Self-Defense of Colombia (AUC) had been formed in the 90s to help combat the killings and extortions carried out by Marxist insurgency groups such as the FARC and the ELN. Though paramilitary operations ceased when the AUC officially disbanded in 2006, since then, the AUC's role as *narcotrafficantes* in the lethal drug trade had grown ever larger.

Kohler's job was to help put a stop to that, a job he'd quickly realized was futile. The Washington/Bogota-backed War on Drugs that started under the Clinton administration not only failed to destroy the Colombian drug trade, but made it even stronger.

There were many reasons for that. One of the primary ones, though, was the CIA/DEA's own role in the proceedings. Selling cocaine was a highly profitable business. People from every side of the equation made sure to get their slice of the pie, and that included Colombian law enforcement and US government agencies.

With his clinical eye, combined with a tireless and ruthless efficiency, Kohler had quickly made himself invaluable, and his input was sought after constantly by both US and Colombian military. However, he was growing tired of his role. A highly-intelligent man with ambitions that stretched way past his modest Army salary, a certain plan had started to foster in his mind, one that would make him a very wealthy man. Over the past few weeks, he'd patiently cultivated the connections he needed to carry it out. Very soon, the last few pieces were about to fall into place.

***

At Tonica Beach, both the mood and the temperature were hot. It was 1:30 a.m. and Kohler sat at a corner table of the busy club. At the front, the dance floor was packed with Colombian party-goers. The men wore colorful T-shirts and flashy wristwatches, while the women wore scanty tops, hot pants, and heels. Mingling among them were several American servicemen, recognizable by their short-sleeved Ben Shermans and cargo pants.

Sitting at the table with Kohler was DEA Special Agent Tony Mackenzie, sweating profusely after a spell on the dance floor. He took a gulp from his rum and Coke, and grinned wolfishly over to where the young lady he'd been dancing with sat with her friend at a nearby table. Curvaceous, ruby-lipped, with long dark hair and flashing eyes, she epitomized the full-bodied sultry looks Colombian women were noted for.

"Man, she is hot!" he exclaimed. "She's got *curvas peligrosas*...dangerous curves. Next dance, I'm going to ask for her number. If she gives it to me, I'll take her home before the night's out."

"Then what do you need her number for?" Kohler said coldly, still irritated from when Mackenzie had sprung up from the table and asked the girl to dance. They had important business at hand, and he was unhappy with the unnecessary diversion.

Mackenzie grinned. "That's how the game is played. Even a farm boy like you ought to know that. You've been here long enough."

Kohler scowled, annoyed how Mackenzie liked to tease him about his rural roots growing up on a farm on the Tennessee/Georgia border. It was unusual for a man in his profession. Besides, all that Latin passion did nothing for the cold-eyed intelligence officer. Unlike his colleague, he had no interest in bedding the local women who hooked up with the gringos. In Colombian slang, they were disdainfully known as *interesadas*, women solely "interested" in one thing. Your wallet.

Kohler would have far preferred to spend the evening on his own, reading a book on military counter-intelligence while Mahler's sixth symphony played in the background. He was at Tonica Beach for a specific purpose, one that allowed him to endure the drunk, moronic behavior of its clientele, including that of the Drug Enforcement Agent sitting opposite him.

He leaned across the table. "I've narrowed our potential candidates to a list of eight. Next week I'm taking some leave and flying out to the East Coast. I'll go to Philadelphia first, then New Jersey if I have to."

Mackenzie's face grew instantly serious. "Do these candidates share a certain fondness for pasta?"

"Yes, all eight."

"Excellent. One of them is going to bite. What we got is too good to turn down. How about here? You take care of the base guards yet?"

Kohler nodded. "They were cheap. Colombian military police don't get paid much."

"How about getting the product onboard the plane? Run that by me again."

"Ten grand gets me thirty minutes alone in the hangar of a C-130 Hercules. It flies to Fort Bliss twice a month, transporting soldiers and couriering back supplies."

"So the pilot is in on this too?"

Kohler shook his head. "He doesn't know a thing. I got one of the ground crew in my pocket. That's all I need."

"You trust him?"

Kohler nodded. "He needs the money. Badly. Besides, if things work out in Philly the way I expect, he'll be in too deep to rat us out."

Mackenzie chuckled. "I'll say. It don't get much deeper than smuggling two hundred bricks of *perico* for the mob," he said, forgetting to keep his customary loud voice low. "His life won't be worth a damn if he screws up."

Kohler frowned, instinctively looking to either side of him. *Perico* was local slang for cocaine. For a DEA agent, Mackenzie was surprisingly loose-lipped, particularly after two rum and Cokes. Nonetheless, it had been his careless and boastful personality that Kohler had unerringly zoomed in on when they'd first met. Something told him the DEA agent shared the same amoral sensibilities as himself.

At times, though, Kohler wondered how Mackenzie had survived this long in a country where DEA agents were routinely executed by the cartels. His looks had helped. Though his father was of Scottish origin, his mother was Puerto Rican. Dark haired with sallow skin, he easily passed as a native Colombian.

He caught Kohler's look. "Chill, Max, it's too noisy for anyone to hear us." He paused a moment. "The Colombian side is a piece of cake. I'm still worried about when the plane lands at Fort Bliss. You sure U.S. Customs agents won't search it?"

Kohler shook his head. "Sometimes they check soldiers' carry-on bags, but never any of the equipment. No sniffer dogs either. All the same, I'm going to wrap fabric softener and plastic-wrap around the product, then put them in ammunition cases. It'll be loaded onto pallets with all the other gear. When it arrives at Fort Bliss, I got a maintenance technician working at the hangar who'll take care of it until I arrive. How about you? You all set?"

Mackenzie picked up his pack of Marlboros off the table and lit a cigarette. He took a long drag, then blew out a ring of smoke. "I finalized my side of the deal this week. We're good to go."

Though he didn't show it, Kohler felt a sense of relief. While he'd studied the logistics of the Colombian drug trade intimately, he had no personal connections within the business. Certainly not for the quantity he intended to smuggle. It was why he'd brought Mackenzie in on the deal. Working undercover, Mackenzie had made numerous connections with the cartels.

"So, where are we sourcing the product? Cali, Medellin, or from the paras?"

Mackenzie blew out another cloud of smoke. "From the paras. Safer that way."

That didn't surprise Kohler. Under Pablo Escobar's rule in the 90s, Medellin had been the center of narcotic operations in the country. Since *El Patron*'s demise, however, the Cali Cartel had taken over. Now it too was in decline, and the disbanded right-wing AUC paramilitaries had taken over large segments of the trade. They'd established their own connections with the Mexican cartels, and were shipping cocaine overland via the Darien Gap, the tiny strip of land that connected South America to Central America.

"I'm tight with a guy named Juan Pablo Mendez," Mackenzie went on. "'Juancho' they call him. He was one of the leaders of the AUC's Northern Bloc. Now he's a top dog in the *Urabenos*. You heard of them, right?"

Kohler nodded. "Sure."

Based in La Guarjira, the *Urabenos* was one of Colombia's most ruthless and ambitious drug trafficking organizations. Located on the country's northeast coastline, the La Guarjira peninsular was a lawless area, long used to smuggle contraband to and from Venezuela. Thirty percent of Colombia's cocaine and heroin passed through there, where it was shipped to Europe via Puerto Caballo. The other way, from Venezuela into Colombia, came cheap gasoline and weapons.

Kohler observed Mackenzie closely. "How well do you know this Juancho?"

Mackenzie grinned. "Real good. We're on party terms."

For decades, DEA agents had worked closely with the Colombian paramilitaries. They provided both military support and intelligence in the DEA's fight against the FARC and ELN. Soon, however, it become clear to everyone that the paras were as deeply involved in the drug trade as the guerrillas. A recent internal report revealed just how close the DEA's relationship had become with them too. Agents had accepted money, weapons, and participated in sex parties funded by the cartels, a scandal that had culminated in the now-infamous congressional hearing. In a country where a low-intensity civil war had been going on for decades, lines of interest had become extremely blurred.

Mackenzie hesitated a moment. "Max, before we go ahead, Juancho wants to meet with you."

Kohler looked at him in surprise. "Me? What for?"

"You're the brains of this operation. Juancho's the kind of guy who needs to know who he's dealing with before he goes into business with them. Besides, you can give him the fifty percent down-payment while you're there."

Kohler frowned. "Are you serious? The Guajira is not the sort of place where carrying a quarter of million dollars in cash is advisable."

"Don't worry. Juancho's men will pick you up in Santa Marta and escort you there. You'll be safe. No one in their right mind is going to fuck with them. They own that turf."

The thought still made Kohler uneasy. "You sure about Juancho?" This time it was Kohler asking the number one question burning on any drug dealer's mind. The issue of trust.

"I've known him for years. We're buddies," Mackenzie assured him. "Besides, this is a new channel for him to export directly into the US. He'd be a fool to turn it down."

Kohler weighed up the situation. Though by no means certain, it didn't make sense for Juancho to leave two hundred and fifty thousand dollars sitting on the table. The odds were he'd make sure to pick up the second half of his money too. But this was Colombia: wild, erratic, and dangerous. Nothing was ever certain in this country.

So…you'll meet him?" Mackenzie pressed him.

"Yeah. I'll meet him. You better be right about him."

Mackenzie looked pleased. "Good. If the Philly trip goes well, I'll make the arrangements as soon as you get back." He drained the last of his drink and stood up from the table. "Now, *parcero*, if you'll excuse me, I'm going to dance. By the time I get back, I'll have that girl's number on a napkin. You know where that leads, don't you?" He grinned lasciviously at Kohler. "*Mi cama.*"

CHAPTER 19

Walter strolled down a well-worn footpath along the west side of the camp. It led to the Conassauga River, where he'd been told he would find Jonah and Billy. Though the day was warm, the clouds were dark gray and the wind had picked up. It looked like a storm was on its way.

For the past two days, he'd had put his micro hydro project on hold. He'd been busy with a series of meetings involving the two camps as the Alaculsy Valley Security Council discussed a range of issues such as communications, perimeter patrols, and joint training exercises. Since their confrontation with Mason, both camps knew just how critical it was to have strict security measures in place. With everything finally agreed on, Walter was ready to build his waterwheel.

"Caught anything?" he asked, arriving down at the riverbank where Jonah and Billy stood with their rods dangling over the water. Ever since he'd introduced them, the two had become as thick as thieves, often joined by Clete whenever there was a fishing expedition to stock the pond.

Billy pointed down at a nearby plastic bucket containing three large brown trout.

"Lunch?" Walter asked. "Or stock?"

"Stock," Billy told him.

"Only another ninety-seven to go, then. Keep going." Walter turned to Jonah. "Remember I said I might need some help with a project I had in mind? Well, I'm starting on it today."

"Yeh mean the micro thingamajig you told me about?"

"Yes, a micro hydro. A waterwheel, to be exact."

"Remind me what that does again?" Jonah asked, reeling in his line.

"It creates electricity, similar to wind energy," Billy cut in before Walter could reply. "Like those big turbines you see on the tops of hills. Only they run on water, not wind."

"Exactly. Was Willow Spring off the grid?" Walter asked, referring to the organic farm Billy had grown up on.

Billy shook his head. "No, but my father hooked up solar and wind power to keep our energy costs down."

"How did that work out?"

"The solar panels worked pretty good. The wind turbine never did much. You sure this waterwheel is going to work? My father used to tell me that before he started any project, he always calculated the R.O..." He stopped, struggling to remember the acronym he was looking for.

"R.O.I.," Walter finished for him. "Return on investment." Walter was impressed yet again by the young boy's knowledge of such matters. "The problem with wind is that it's an unreliable source of power, and doesn't work well in small-scale setups. The creek I intend using will supply us with constant power. I've already built a dam to increase the water pressure. So, Jonah, you interested in helping out? Ned told me it was okay to steal you for a few days. The waterwheel ought to generate enough power for both our communities."

"Deffo. A bit of light in the evenings would be a grand thing. Only I don't do anything these days without me wingman, Billy the Kid." Jonah winked at Walter. "Yeh get two for the price of one when yeh sign me up."

Walter shook his head. "The project will involve using electric saws and other power tools. They're too dangerous for Billy to be anywhere near."

A disappointed look came over Billy's face. "But—"

"It's okay, Walter," Jonah said. "I'll see to it the lad doesn't handle anything other than manual tools. Sure, in the old days they used to send kids his age down the mines and up the chimneys. He won't be doing anything *that* dangerous."

Walter hesitated. He liked Jonah, but was unsure how well he would manage the young boy. *Responsible* and *mature* weren't exactly the first words that came to mind when describing the excitable Irishman. The last thing he wanted was for Billy to be involved in a serious accident.

"Please…" Billy pleaded. "I really want to help."

"All right," Walter reluctantly agreed. He looked down at the boy sternly. "Just promise me, you'll let Jonah handle the electric saw."

"Promise!"

"The only one losing his fingers in the chop saw will be me," Jonah assured Walter.

Walter shook his head. "Come down to the workshop tomorrow morning and we'll get started." With that, he set off and headed back up the footpath again, pleased with how everything had panned out. The one downside was the extra pressure he was putting himself under. Building a waterwheel was a difficult undertaking. He wasn't entirely sure if he would succeed.

CHAPTER 20

At 8:30 a.m. the following morning, Walter headed over to his workshop. It was a bright, sunny day without a cloud in the sky. The previous night, there had been a ferocious thunderstorm that had lasted several hours. The weather had cleared, and the sky was a deep blue once again.

When he arrived, Jonah and Billy were already waiting for him. "Just like old times," he said as he unlocked the barn door.

He took them over to the workbench they'd used previously. Along the sidewall were the chop saw and the miter saw he'd picked up in Home Depot. The two machines were plugged into an extension cable that ran to the back of the barn, where he'd placed the propane generator. Walter quickly showed Jonah how to use it, then took him over to the cabinet where he kept the carpentry tools. Inside was a multitude of handsaws: a rip saw, a crosscut saw, and several back saws, including a dovetail, carcass, and tenon saw.

"Why don't you explain to Billy the need for all these," he told Jonah, curious to see exactly what the Irishman knew about carpentry. He was soon satisfied as Jonah patiently explained to Billy the uses of each saw, the dovetail saw with its fine rip teeth for cutting joinery *along* the grain, the carcass saw for cutting *across* the grain, the larger tenon saw for deeper cuts, and so on.

"Right, Walter," the Irishman said when he'd finished. "Ye've got four willing hands at yer disposal. What do yeh want us to do?"

Walter pointed to a stack of chunky two-by-six boards a few feet away. "I got these from a redwood deck I dismantled in Old Fort the other day. It was quicker than visiting a lumberyard. We're going to use it to build the waterwheel. The age-weathered wood will look nice too." He paused briefly. "Before we start, I'm going to give you both a quick lesson on how we produce hydroelectricity. That way, you'll have an idea what we're trying to achieve here."

"Does it involve maths?" Jonah asked worriedly. "Other than measuring angles, it's not exactly me strongest suit."

"Nope, no maths. Simply put, we're going to build a device capable of converting the energy of moving water to electrical energy, known as kinetic energy, and is measured by the volume of water and the vertical interval through which it falls." He caught Jonah's blank stare. "In other words, how much water flows down the river and the height from which it drops."

"I get it. The more water and the further it drops, the more power we'll get from the waterwheel, that right?"

"Exactly. And the more efficiently we build the wheel, the faster it'll turn."

"When I was a kid, me dad attached a dynamo lamp to the back wheel of me bicycle," Jonah mused. "When I pedaled hard, the lights came on. I always thought it pure magic."

Walter smiled. "Yes, nature's magic, and the waterwheel works on a similar principle. In this case, the dynamo I intend using will be a car alternator, which I'll convert to a permanent magnet alternator to maximize the power we draw from the wheel."

Jonah's face clouded over again. "Yeh have me head spinning already, professor. Look, you work on the magic, me and Billy will build yer wheel." He pointed impatiently to the notebook in Walter's hand that he'd opened to the design of the waterwheel. "Give us a gander at that and we'll get cracking."

"All right, enough with the theory." Walter placed the notebook down on the workbench and gathered the two around him. For the next few minutes, he gave them a brief rundown on how the waterwheel would be constructed, using a series of detailed sketches he'd drawn. Four feet in diameter, it was comprised of two identical outer wheels, in between which eight buckets would be built to capture the water and turn the device on its center hub. Walter was confident it would harness enough energy for their needs.

"Some waterwheels are built with ten spokes. We're only going to build eight. That way, it makes the carpentry easier. No difficult angles to measure."

Jonah, who had been paying close attention, immediately understood. "Got yeh. I can use the standard settings on the miter saw for those angles. Nothing finicky."

"Exactly." So far, Walter was impressed with the Irishman. He appeared to know exactly what he needed to do. The proof was in the pudding, however. He'd find out soon enough what sort of waterwheel got built.

After going through the specifications, he assembled the tools Jonah and Billy would require, including a cordless drill, a sixteen gauge finish nailer, a tape measure, and a speed square.

"All right, get to work. I'll be over at my workbench rigging up the alternator."

Jonah rubbed his hands. "Right, lad," he said to Billy. "We'll start by building the spokes." He glanced down at Walter's design and jotted some notes. "Let's see, each wheel has one center spoke, two cross spokes, and four intermediate spokes. No bother, I'll show yeh how to measure the wood, then I'll cut it to size. How does that grab yeh?"

"Can I cut some pieces with a handsaw?" Billy asked.

"'Course yeh can. But see, this wood is old, we need to prepare it first." Jonah picked up one of the lengths of two-by-sixes. Examining it, he removed the leftover nails with a claw hammer. "Make sure to get all of them out, or yeh'll banjax the saw blades. Walter will have a fit and chuck the two of us out of here."

Over at his workbench, Walter grinned, pleased to see Jonah's paternal concern for the young boy. Despite his constant joking, it was plain to see that he had no intention of allowing Billy to do anything dangerous.

Once he'd gotten all the nails out, Jonah showed Billy how to measure the wood for the first center spoke, using the good part from the middle, then he switched on the chop saw and cut off the marked ends.

Other than the center spoke, all other cuts were under two feet, making perfect use of the old redwood deck. The two cross spokes were simple to make, and only required the chop saw to cut them to length. The intermediate spokes were harder. Once cut to size, one end of each needed to be cut to a forty-five-degree angle using the miter saw. With Billy's precise measurements and Jonah's abundant energy, the spokes for both wheels were quickly made.

"Time to put these babies together," Jonah told Billy once the pieces for both wheels had been prepared. "We'll see how good yer measurements are."

He placed one of the center spokes on the floor, then he and Billy attached the two cross spokes on either side with wood glue. With the drill, Jonah countersunk three-inch deck screws to attach them firmly in place.

The pointed intermediate spokes were fitted next, slotted into the four corners of the cross. They fit perfectly.

"Spot on, fella, yeh measured them bang on!" Jonah said delightedly. "Righty ho, let's put the second wheel together, then it's onto the paddles and outer rims."

While they worked, Walter was deep in his own efforts, modifying the Camry's alternator to a permanent magnet alternator.

In previous projects, he'd always used a ready-built PMA, and he was a little apprehensive about building one from scratch. And without the modification, they wouldn't harness enough energy from the slow-moving waterwheel to generate sufficient electricity. He thought about Billy's comment the previous day. If he couldn't build the PMA, the project would be deep in negative ROI. He smiled grimly to himself at what the serious-minded Billy Bingham might think of that.

The Camry's alternator had been produced for the Toyota 22R engine, and was probably the most common model in the world. Walter started off by removing its back cover, held in place with three screws, then removed all the exposed parts sitting above the inner casing: the voltage regulator, brushes, and rectifier. Once they were out, he carefully unscrewed the inner casing, exposing the rotor and stator.

Removing the rotor was difficult. He needed to clamp the alternator to the bench vise and use a socket wrench to wrestle it loose. Then he removed the stator, which came out a little easier.

Now he was ready to modify the rotor to use his rare-earth magnets. He glued each magnet onto the core, placing them around the spindle so that they were alternately arrayed with opposing poles. It was painstaking work and took over an hour. When he was done, he re-attached the rotor inside the casing, then stood up and stretched his back, sore from stooping over.

"How yeh getting on?" Jonah asked, observing him from the other side of the room. "Any joy yet?"

Walter shook his head. "Too soon to tell. To be honest, I'm having trouble figuring this out. Hopefully I can get it going okay."

Jonah and Billy both stared at him. "Hopefully? Me and Billy are working like blue-arse flies here," Jonah said sternly. "Yeh telling us it's all for nothing?"

"Of course not. It's just a little trickier than I thought, that's all."

"Why? It's not like yer reinventing the wheel or anything."

"Yeah, right," Walter said testily, ignoring the Irishman's joke. Pencil in hand, he leaned over and made a calculation in his notebook, his brow furrowed with concentration.

Jonah chuckled. "Yeh remind me of a constipated mathematician with that look on yer face. Yeh know how he figured it out, don't yeh?"

"No. How?"

"He worked it out with his pencil."

It took Walter a moment to get the joke. Unable to help himself, he straightened up, laughing hard. "Thanks, Jonah. That just made my day!"

Lifted by Jonah's wisecracking, Walter set about rewiring the stator, rewinding it in a three-phase pattern so that it was compatible with the newly-installed magnets.

Jonah and Billy had moved onto building the axle for the waterwheel. While Billy held one of the Camry's wheel bearing hubs in place, Jonah screwed it onto one of the wheels, then after fitting the threaded rod, the two screwed on the second hub.

They stood back and admired their work. "Looks like she's ready to spin," Jonah remarked once he'd finished tightening everything up. He looked across the room. "Walter, are yeh done yet?"

"Nearly there," Walter grunted, still busy rewiring the stator. It was intricate work, and it took him over an hour to complete.

When it was ready, he spent the next thirty minutes re-installing the rest of the components before finally screwing on the alternator's back cover.

116

"Done," he said, wiping his brow. "Time to test this sucker."

He grabbed his volt meter and attached the positive end of the tester onto the copper end of the rectifier, protruding out of the alternator's casing. After placing the negative end against the metal cover, he grabbed a piece of cord and used it to turn the pulley attached at the front of the alternator.

He glanced down at the volt meter. It registered twelve volts. A wide smile came over his face.

"So, we in business?" Jonah called out.

Walter tugged the rope back and forth even faster. The volt meter registered thirteen volts. He let go of the rope and looked over to where Jonah and Billy had stopped working and were staring anxiously at him. "Oh, yeah. We're in business."

"Magic!" Jonah rubbed his hands gleefully. "So what are we waiting for? Let's haul everything up to the river and put it to the test!"

CHAPTER 21

Tiffany Parker woke up to sound of leaves rustling outside her tent. She bolted upright and stuck her head out through the flap. Was it just an animal? She peered nervously into the forest. Ever since arriving at Lake Ocoee, her senses had been on full alert. She was a city girl, and hadn't gone camping since she was a kid. Tiffany had hated it then, though not nearly as much as she hated it now.

"Guys, I think somebody's out there!" she hissed to her companions on either side of her. "I'm not kidding," she added when no one replied. It was a baking hot afternoon, and everyone was dozing after lunch. To her right, Dan and Jade slept together in their two-man tent, the flaps open to let in the breeze, while on the other side, Higgs and Cornel slept on blankets outside theirs.

The group of five had arrived at Lake Ocoee that morning, and had set up camp at a small clearing three miles east of Devil's Point. The area was surrounded by thick forest, and they'd had to trek five hundred yards from the highway to reach it. Any location with good road access, or that had a jetty had all been taken, and their options had been limited. That had surprised Tiffany. When they'd left Atlanta two days ago, the city was a ghost town. She hadn't expected there to be so many people at the lake.

It hadn't surprised Jade Woo though, the other girl in the group. Before the pandemic, she had been a third-year computer science engineer. "Why would you think otherwise?" she'd asked Tiffany scornfully. "Tennessee had a population of six million. The survival rate for vPox is around two percent. Simple math tells you that there must be well over a hundred thousand people wandering about the state."

Tiffany had remained silent. She didn't do math. Not even the simple kind.

"Damn, that's a lot of people!" Karl Higgs said, raising an eyebrow in surprise. His math obviously wasn't that great either. Higgs was the unspoken leader of the group. He was an asshole too, and had been hitting on Tiffany ever since she joined the group the day before leaving Atlanta. Though tall, he had an ungainly figure and a lumbering gait, ginger hair and small pig eyes. Tiffany had zero interest in him. As well as math, she didn't do ugly. Not even in these times.

"That's going to change fast, though," Jade had continued. "Once basic meds and bottled water run out, secondary mortalities will kick in, such as pre-existing illnesses and opportunistic diseases. There's a lot of sick people in this country. They're not going to make it."

"Yes, but we'll make it," Higgs said firmly. "We're young, healthy, and strong. We'll stay that way too, so long as we keep making the right decisions. Speaking of which, I say tomorrow we move on and look for a better location. This sucks here. Everyone cool with that?"

Everybody had looked at each other and nodded. No one bothered to look at Tiffany. As far as decisions went, she didn't register. A "spoiled, useless bitch," Higgs had called her that day when he hadn't gotten his way. He'd even threatened to kick her out of the group. If not for the fact that Cornel had stood up for her, he might have done so. Dark-skinned, slightly-built, with cornrows that ran tightly down the back of his head, Cornel was the only one who was nice to her. Normally quiet and introspective, she'd been surprised he'd stuck up for her. Grateful too.

In truth, though, Tiffany *was* spoiled. Or at least, she used to be. As an only child growing up in the affluent Atlanta neighborhood of Morningside, she'd become adept in manipulating her parents from an early age, and was rarely denied anything she ever asked for, particularly from her father. That same skill had transferred smoothly over in later life. Prior to the pandemic, she'd been living with her thirty-two-year-old boyfriend, Paul Hariri, and had enjoyed a comfortable existence in their luxury, sixteen-hundred-square-foot condominium at Cumberland Heights, overlooking the river.

Of Lebanese descent, Paul came from a wealthy family that owned businesses all over the US. Seven years her senior, he'd been a property developer, and drove around Atlanta in a Lexus convertible. Sometimes he took Tiffany with him to meet clients. Her presence helped disarm certain personality types, he explained to her once; brash young men who might otherwise negotiate more aggressively with him. Privately, Tiffany suspected he just liked showing her off to fellow brash young men. Not that she minded. With natural blonde hair and a toned, shapely body that she worked hard in the gym to keep that way - the only "work" she'd ever done in her life - Tiffany was exceptionally beautiful, and loved to be admired by men. In her experience, women tended not to like her quite so much, however.

Tragically, her pampered lifestyle was over. Paul had died a torturous death between the luxurious Egyptian cotton sheets of their huge bed. By the time he drew his last breath, he was unrecognizable, a grotesque pus-filled monstrosity that filled her with revulsion. It had been a nightmare. The thought that her own exquisite features would soon suffer the same fate terrified her, and on more than one occasion she'd been tempted to run away. Only, there had been nowhere to run. Everywhere in the city, people were suffering similar fates. Even her parents had come down with the deadly virus, and her father had warned her away from visiting the house.

Miraculously, she hadn't come down with vPox. She was somehow immune to the disease. She now suffered a different type of fate, as an unpopular, bedraggled figure with unwashed hair and mosquito-bitten arms, with people like Jade and Higgs for company. It was so unfair.

Behind her came the sound of more rustling. It was even closer this time. She craned her neck around the side of the tent and stared into the forest. "Guys, I'm serious. Someone is out there!"

"You said that earlier," Jade called out grumpily.

Next to her, Dan barely stirred. He was the most handsome in the group, and he and Jade had hooked up the day before Tiffany joined them. She suspected Jade's attitude toward her was because she felt threatened. She couldn't think of any other reason. Small and lithe, Jade was by no means unattractive, but she certainly wasn't as pretty as Tiffany. No way.

"Yes, but I hear—"

"So what?" Jade snapped. "We're in a forest teeming with wildlife. I told you, there's no gangs here like in the cities, just ordinary people like us. We're away from all that now. There's no gas stations or supermarkets to control. What would be the point?"

Tiffany wasn't so sure. The men at the last camp they'd passed that morning had looked a rough lot. One of them, a skinny man with lank brown hair and two missing front teeth, had leered at her as she walked by, cajoling her to tell him her name. She'd ignored him and looked the other way, prompting a tirade of foul words to spew from his lips.

Outside his tent, Higgs lifted his head sleepily and called out to her. "Tiffany, stop looking for attention. If you're feeling lonely, just say the word and you can snuggle up here beside me. I'll keep you safe." Tiffany could see Higgs's eyes moistening at the thought, and shuddered.

On her other side, Jade chuckled. "Karl's not such a bad guy. You should take him up on that. After all, you won't find many people willing to look after such a princess these days."

Dan rolled onto his back and sniggered.

Princess. That was the term Jade had come up with for her shortly after she'd joined the group. It had been her own fault. She'd found it hard to adapt to her new circumstances, and had complained incessantly. Now everyone except Cornel called her that. She shook her head in frustration. If there was one thing she would change if given the chance, it was how spoiled she'd behaved when she'd initially met everyone. It was too late now. Her status as princess was set in stone.

Behind her, a single shot rang out. "Nobody move!" a harsh, guttural voice yelled out. "We got you surrounded!"

Tiffany jerked her head around to see four men emerge from the forest. Spread several feet apart, all had rifles raised to their shoulders, and walked quickly toward them.

"Karl, get up!" Dan shouted in alarm. He rummaged around in his tent, then came charging out through the flaps. Several shots rang out in quick succession. Inside the tent, Jade screamed in agony.

Dan spun around and darted back inside the tent "My God! Jade's been hit!" he cried out frantically. "Please…stop shooting!"

"Goddammit, I said nobody move!" the man shouted again. "Everybody out of the tents. One at a time, with your hands in the air!"

Her heart pounding, Tiffany crawled out of her tent. She stood up and raised her arms. Behind her, the men approached warily through the grasses. When they reached the edge of the clearing, one grinned wickedly at her, displaying two missing front teeth. "Hello darling. How's my little pretty one? Ready for some fun?"

Tiffany felt dizzy, like she was about to faint.

A few feet away, Dan got out of his tent. He looked stricken. He reached back inside and dragged Jade out gently by the arms. There was a large red stain on one side of her T-shirt, just above her waist, and her shorts were splattered with blood. Her eyes fluttered, and she moaned weakly.

One of the intruders scowled, a large bearded man with a beer belly, wearing a checked red shirt and brown hiking shorts. "Jeb, you damn idiot. You've gone shot one of the bitches."

The skinny man with missing front teeth pointed at Dan. "That fucker was about to shoot at us, Kurt," he said in an aggrieved tone. "How the hell was I to know she was inside?"

Outside the tent, Dan knelt beside Jade. He'd grabbed a fresh T-shirt and was applying it to her wound, desperately trying to staunch the flow of blood that continued to pump out.

Kurt focused his attention on Higgs next, who stood alongside Cornel. While Cornel maintained an impassive air, Higgs looked scared to death. His eyes rolled wildly around in their sockets as he gaped at the intruders. From the outset, he'd made no attempt to reach for his rifle, which lay on the ground by entrance to his tent.

"Hey, big guy. You the leader of this group?" Kurt asked. "Looked that way earlier, strutting past us like you were some kind of tough guy."

"No...we-we don't have a leader," Higgs stammered, his legs trembling badly.

"I see. Y'all just good friends, that it?" Kurt pointed at Tiffany. "So how come blondie here is all on her own? Don't she have any friends?"

A few yards away, Jeb chuckled. "She'll have some new friends soon enough. Won't she, Kurt?"

Kurt ignored his toothless companion and continued to stare at Tiffany keenly. "So what's your name, blondie? Jeb asked you earlier, but you wouldn't talk to him. Can't say I blame you, he's just an ugly runt." He puffed out his chest, grinning. "Now me, I'm one handsome *hombre*. You can tell me."

All four intruders, including Jeb, laughed loudly. Tiffany stood there, petrified, unable to answer. The nightmare of the last few weeks had just gotten indefinably worse. Some part of her still hoped this was just a bad dream. That any moment she would wake up to find herself in her big comfortable bed beside a fit and healthy Paul, and she could get back to her cosseted life instead of this horror show.

"I said what's your name, goddammit," Kurt repeated gruffly. "Don't make me come over and slap it out of you."

"Tiffany," she finally managed to get out.

Kurt smiled sweetly at her. "Tiffany? Now that's a nice name. All right, Tiffany, go inside your tent and pack up your stuff. You're coming with me."

Tiffany blinked hard. "With you...where?"

"Back to my *hacienda*, of course. Unless your friends have any objections, that is?" Kurt glanced at Higgs and Cornel, then across at Dan, who was still tending to Jade. It appeared he'd managed to stop the bleeding, and was talking to her in a low, urgent voice. She sat on the grass with her head resting limply against his shoulder, her eyes darting anxiously from one intruder to the other.

Jeb looked over at her. "Kurt, how about the cute little Asian? We taking her back too?"

Kurt nodded. "You break it, you buy it. She's all yours."

Jeb strolled over to where Jade now sat upright in alarm. "Aw, she's not broken too bad. Looks like her boyfriend's patched her up good."

Dan rose to his feet. "Keep away from her, you animal!" he snarled. Before he'd even fully straightened up, Jeb raised his rifle and shot him twice in the chest. With a grunt, Dan fell backward into Jade's lap.

She screamed hysterically. "Dan! No!" She desperately tried to revive him, but to no avail. Dan had died almost instantly.

Jeb looked down at her with a crooked grin. "Get up, cutie. You're coming with—" His voice broke off as something caught his attention. He stared past Jade, into the forest. "Jesus H Christ," he muttered in amazement. "What the fuck is that?"

Tiffany looked over to where he was staring. Her eyes widened when a man stepped out of the forest and walked quickly toward them. In his hands he held a crossbow, pointed toward the ground, but what startled her the most was his appearance. Bare-chested, with a tanned, muscular torso. A narrow strip of blond hair ran down the middle of his otherwise shaved scalp.

My God, she thought in amazement. *There must have been an Indian reservation somewhere around here. This is one of the survivors.* Then, a second thought crossed her mind. *What on Earth does he want?*

CHAPTER 22

Walter, Jonah, and Billy hauled the waterwheel and its components up to the creek. The wheel, now attached to its axle and bearings, was extremely heavy, and they used a modified supermarket cart (the end hacked off and its side grills pulled back) to push it up the track. By the time they reached the creek, they were breathing heavily.

"*Jaysus*, I wouldn't want to do that again in a hurry," Jonah said, wiping his brow with the back of his hand. He looked around. "Where are we going to put this contraption?"

Walter pointed over to the section of the creek just below where he'd built the dam. "Right there, but first we got to haul up some wood to house the wheel. Oh, and we need to build a spillway, to channel the water into the buckets."

"Yeh what?" Jonah said looking at him in mock horror. "If we'd known that, we'd have charged yeh a higher rate for the work, wouldn't we, Billy?"

"Double," Billy deadpanned, who'd cottoned onto Jonah's ways by now.

Walter grinned. "Which is exactly why I didn't. Too late now."

An hour and a half later, the three had constructed a simple trestle-shaped platform to support the waterwheel.

Walter was grateful to have Jonah working alongside him. As well as being an excellent carpenter, the brawny Irishman was a natural problem-solver too, and his constant wisecracking made the time go all the faster.

When it was ready, they straddled the platform across the stream and fixed it securely in place. Walter and Jonah lifted the wheel out of the cart, and with Billy hollering out instructions, splashed clumsily around in the creek until they managed to slot either side of the axle into the metal mounts they'd attached to the platform.

Gasping for air, the three admired their work. "Go on, Billy," Jonah urged the boy. "Give it a whirl. I dare yeh."

Billy stepped forward. Gripping one of the paddles with both hands, he pushed down hard. The wheel turned slowly. Jonah gave it a few slaps, and soon it was spinning fast. "*Yee ha!*" he shouted. "Look at that baby go!"

Walter looked on with satisfaction. "You guys did a hell of a job. Well done!"

Grinning at each other, Jonah and Billy high-fived with a resounding slap.

"All right," Walter said. "It's not time to rest on your laurels yet. We still need to build the spillway. After that, we got to assemble the gearing and connect the wheel to the alternator."

"No peace for the wicked," Jonah grumbled. "Not even a cup of tea and a crumbly biscuit for our efforts."

The waterwheel was an "overshot" design. It meant that the spillway needed to come over the top so that the water plunged down the far side, spinning the wheel in the same direction as the stream. Walter placed a brick across the gap in the dam so that they could work without being soaked. He and Jonah took some measurements and commenced building the trough that would channel the water as it poured over the drop, along with a long-legged platform to support it.

Once everything had been put in place, from below, Walter shouted up to the top of the damn where Billy was waiting. "All right, let her rip!"

Billy leaned over and lifted out the brick. With a loud gurgle, the water rushed down the spillway. Moments later it spilled over the edge and dropped five feet below to where the waterwheel was positioned.

The wheel slowly started to turn, then picked up speed. All three cheered, the grins on their faces even larger than before.

"It'll spin slower once the load from the alternator is attached," Walter said. "But this is going to fly." He signaled for Billy to replace the brick again.

It took over an hour to assemble the gearing components and attach them to the wheel. From a racing bike Walter had picked up, Jonah deftly dismantled the front sprocket, roller chain, and rear wheel, complete with the hub gear attached. Stripping off the back tire, Walter fit the Camry's serpentine belt over the rim, then he and Jonah connected everything to the alternator.

Once Walter was satisfied with the configuration, Billy raced up the side of the creek and lifted out the brick again. The water came gushing down the trough, and the wheel began to turn, slower this time, carrying the load from the alternator.

"I'd say that's creating enough juice to run everything we need at the farm," Walter estimated. From his toolkit, he produced a boat light. As soon as he'd attached it to the alternator, it shone brightly, even in the daylight.

Jonah slapped him on the back. "Walter, yer a bleedin' genius, so yeh are!" he exclaimed, grinning like a loon. "To be honest, I had me doubts whether this contraption would ever work."

"Me too," Walter replied, grinning too.

Billy came scrambling down the hill to join them. "Wow!" he said, his eyes shining almost as strongly as the boat lamp. "That...that's..."

"Pure magic," Jonah said to the sound of water sloshing noisily into the waterwheel's buckets.

"Nature's magic," Walter corrected him. "I still need to run a connection back to the farmhouse and figure out where to get a transformer, but that's for another day. We've done the hard part."

"Absolutely," Jonah agreed. "Time to put the kettle on and break out the biscuits. I might even skip the tea and have a beer to celebrate." He grinned. "Don't tell Colleen. She'll go through me for a shortcut drinking this early."

Walter draped an arm over his shoulder. "We won't say a word, will we, Billy? I might even join you. Thirsty work building a waterwheel, and beer beats tea any day of the week."

CHAPTER 23

The American Indian strode through the grasses toward Tiffany and the others. When he got to within fifty yards, she noted that he carried a pistol at his waist. Glancing down at his feet, she saw he was barefoot.

All conversation had ceased. Jeb, who stood next to Jade, still holding the lifeless Dan in her arms, said to Kurt in amazement, "Just when you thought the world had run out of surprises, this guy shows—"

He was cut off mid-stream, his words replaced by a gurgling sound as a two-foot arrow lodged in the side of his neck and protruded out the other side. Clutching his throat, he dropped to his knees, uttering something incomprehensible.

Before anyone could react, a shot rang out. A chunk of Kurt's head instantly disappeared, and a film of pink mist sprayed into the air. With a brief grunt, the big man collapsed to the ground.

Two more shots followed in quick succession, and the man guarding Karl and Cornel dropped to one knee, clutching his stomach. Another shot hit him in the chest and he keeled over.

Tiffany spun around to see a second man step out from another part of the forest. He was also bare-chested, also with a bleached Mohawk. Though bigger than the first Indian, he was less toned. "Drop your weapon!" he yelled at the last surviving intruder.

The startled man did as he was told, and raised his hands in the air.

The first Indian walked into the camp, his crossbow reloaded and raised at eye level. When he got closer, Tiffany saw that, although deeply tanned, he was a white man, not Native American. It only added to her confusion.

He stopped ten feet away from the last surviving man, staring at him with a disturbing intensity.

"L-Look, mister, I don't want no more trouble," the intruder stuttered. "Please, just let me go…that okay?"

The Mohawked stranger shook his head, then squeezed the trigger of the crossbow. An arrow whizzed through the air and buried itself in the man's heart. He staggered back, clutching the arrow with one hand, and collapsed wordlessly onto his back.

Tiffany pulled her eyes away from him and gazed at the stranger. Above his right temple was a small hole. It was about the size of quarter and had a nasty, dark scab over it. A recent bullet wound, she guessed.

"Wh-who are you?" she asked. Still in shock, she had no idea what else to say.

"Your savior," the man replied. "Hurry up. You need to pack your things."

"Why?" Tiffany asked, totally confused.

The man prodded a toe at the dead man splayed out on the ground before him. "The men from his camp will have heard the shooting. It's too risky to stay here."

"But where will we go?"

"To my camp. You'll be safe there."

Tiffany hesitated, unsure whether to trust this bizarre-looking stranger. Something about his assured manner made her feel safe, however, in a way Higgs most certainly didn't. Besides, it wasn't as if she had many options right now. "All right," she said. "Which way?"

CHAPTER 24

The group of six hiked single-file through thick forest. Almost as soon as they left the camp, Tiffany completely lost her bearings. Whether they were heading parallel to the lake shore or away from it, she had no idea; she just followed the American Indian, who led the way. Without knowing anything about him, what else was she to think of him as?

Carrying her pack on her shoulders, it was hard to keep up with him. Apart from his head wound, he appeared incredibly healthy. A light film of sweat covered his muscular torso, and though barefoot, his gait was steady and surefooted as he navigated the tangled overgrowth of the forest floor.

Behind her, Higgs and Cornel had a harder job keeping up. As well as their backpacks, they carried Jade on a stretcher made from two sturdy branches, between which her nylon tent had been attached. There had been no time to bury Dan; the Indians had insisted they leave right away. Before parting, Jade tearfully kissed him on the forehead, then lay down on the stretcher and turned her head away.

After ten minutes of brisk walking, Tiffany quickened her step so that she was only a couple of yards behind the first Indian. They had separated from the rest of the group as

Higgs and the slightly-built Cornel struggled to keep up the pace.

"Everything happened so fast back there, I haven't had a chance to thank you yet," Tiffany said between breaths. "By the way, my name is Tiffany. What's yours?"

"Chris," the man said without turning around.

"And your friend?"

"Mark."

Tiffany felt slightly disappointed by their commonplace names. They should have changed them to something more *tribal*. "We're so lucky you were close by when those brutes attacked us. God knows what would have happened if you hadn't."

"It wasn't luck. We've been watching you since this morning."

Tiffany stopped in her tracks, then hurried forward again when Chris continued without stopping. "You've been following us?"

Chris nodded. "We were spying on the settler camp when you passed by. Soon as you left, those four men followed you."

"And you followed them...why?"

"You saw what they came for. I wasn't going to stand for that. Now that you're with my tribe, you'll be safe."

"How many are in your tribe?" Tiffany asked. The thought of a dozen bare-chested men with crazy haircuts waiting to whoop their arrival made her a little uneasy.

Chris counted briefly under his breath. "Six."

"I see. Are they waiting for you back at your camp?"

Chris shook his head. "No, everyone is here with me."

Tiffany's step faltered as she took in the implication of Chris's words. "Y-You mean us?"

"Yes. The four of you are with me now. You won't survive otherwise."

***

For the rest of the journey, Tiffany remained quiet, mulling over what Chris had said. Both his appearance and the way he'd flatly presumed she and the others were now part of his tribe suggested that something was deeply wrong with him. Nonetheless, neither he nor Mark had threatened them in any way and were clearly helping them.

She wondered whether Chris's head injury had something to do with his behavior. She'd read somewhere that brain damage could affect a person's personality without necessarily diminishing their faculties. That wouldn't account for Mark, though he didn't appear particularly bright. Perhaps he'd known Chris prior to his injury and had remained with him, she reasoned. When it came to friendships, there weren't too many choices these days, something she was painfully aware of. And despite everything, there was something about Chris's self-assuredness and intense gaze that demanded he be taken seriously. One way or another, Tiffany was determined to figure it out. She was good at things like that.

The journey took well over an hour, the latter part over hilly terrain. They were taking the longer, but easier, route, Chris informed her, so that Jade could be carried. Even so, Higgs and Cornel had to rest several times. Tiffany was surprised to see that Higgs was clearly the more exhausted of the two. He puffed hard, and sweat poured off his face. Though lighter in build, Cornel's wiry frame was obviously the more resilient.

Finally, they climbed around the side of a hill and crested one of its lower ridges. Below was a lightly-wooded valley. Chris stopped, and pointed down to where a copse of tall trees nestled on its lower slopes next to a river. "There's my camp," he said.

Tiffany scrunched her eyes, but couldn't make anything out. Before she could reply, Chris stepped over the edge and down a rocky slope. She followed after him, and soon they were among the larches and pines, walking down a forest track. Before they reached the river, Chris turned off the trail and zig-zagged his way through the trees. Ahead, Tiffany started to make out various hues of greens and browns. Only when she was fifteen feet away could she finally make out the camp.

Built in a clearing among the trees, it was neat and perfunctory. She passed a fire pit lined with stones, upon which a pot sat on top of a metal grill. Nearby was a small hut covered by a plastic tarp. Peering inside it, she saw several pots and pans and a couple of large plastic containers. Outside, several propane tanks were neatly lined up in a row beside a gas stove. This was obviously the camp's kitchen area.

Chris walked past it and headed toward where a large canvas tent was suspended between the branches of two trees. Nearby, clothes were drying on a line. Tiffany noted how nothing brightly-colored had been left out that might attract attention. A person could easily walk within ten feet of the camp without noticing it.

Chris threw back one of the tent flaps and beckoned Tiffany forward. She stepped past him and entered. Looking around, she was surprised to see how roomy it was inside, cool too. The roof, though sagging slightly, was over eight feet high, and there was no need to stoop. She estimated that the total area was around two hundred square feet. During her time with Paul Hariri, she'd become adept in calculating the floor spaces of kitchens, bedrooms, and bathrooms. A tent was no harder to estimate.

In opposing corners were foam mattresses with neatly-folded sleeping bags on each, and in the middle of the room was a tree stump that served as a table. On it stood a jug, filled with water, along with several plastic tumblers stacked on their backs.

Chris walked over to it and poured out a cup. He handed it to Tiffany. The water tasted cool and clean, and she gratefully drank it in a few thirsty mouthfuls.

"How long have you been here?" she asked, placing the tumbler back down on the stump.

"We moved here three days ago. Our last location wasn't suitable."

"In what way?"

"In many ways. For a start, it was too close to the settlers."

"Then why were you spying on their camp today?" Tiffany asked curiously. "Are they your enemies?"

Chris shook his head. "To steal supplies from them."

"Oh...I see. Isn't that better to do at night?"

"Yes, but first you need to find out what to take. That's easier to do during the day."

At that moment, Mark arrived, followed by a weary Higgs and Cornel. Chris pointed to the bed in the far corner. "Take her there," he told them.

The two carried Jade over and laid her on the ground beside the bed, then gently lifted her out of the stretcher and onto the mattress.

Even with the flaps open, it was gloomy inside the tent. Chris grabbed a flashlight from off the top of a nearby box, then squatted beside Jade. He took her pulse. "Good," he said after a few moments.

He lifted her T-shirt above her waist, and removed the blood-soaked cloth that Dan had applied to the wound. He angled the flashlight at it and inspected it carefully, then gently turned her over onto her side and examined her back.

"What are you doing?" Cornel asked. He and Tiffany stood at the end of the bed to get a better view.

"I'm looking to see if there's an exit wound. There's none. The bullet is still inside her."

Chris stood up and stretched one foot over the bed so that his feet were on either side of Jade's waist. "Give me your hands," he told her.

Jade looked up at him apprehensively.

"Don't worry, I won't hurt you."

After a moment's hesitation, Jade raised her hands. Chris took them in his, then stepped back slowly so that her torso lifted off the bed. After a few inches, Jade winced.

"Where does it hurt?" Chris asked her.

"Deep inside. My liver, I think."

"How about your back? Does it feel okay?"

Jade nodded. "I think so."

"Move it from side to side…slowly."

Jade did as she was told and carefully rotated her hips. "You mean like that?"

"Yes, that's good." Chris lowered her down onto the bed again, looking pleased.

Now Tiffany understood why Chris had gotten Jade to move. He was testing whether she had sustained a spinal injury. "How about internal bleeding?" she asked. "Is there any way to tell?"

"I doubt there's any. If there was, she'd be dead by now. She'd have bled out."

That made sense, and any lingering doubts Tiffany had about Chris's mental capacity disappeared. "Are you going to remove the bullet?" she asked.

"I don't have the instruments," Chris replied. "Even if I did, that's not necessarily a good thing to do. Best thing she can do is rest up and let her injury heal."

"What about infection?"

Chris shook his head. "Even in modern medicine, bullets aren't usually removed unless they're obstructing something vital. If there's any infection, we can treat it with antibiotics. I'll just clean the wound and bandage her up properly. Mark! Bring me the medicine bag."

A few moments later, Mark came over to the bed with a jute tote bag. Chris rummaged around it and took out a pair of scissors, a white plastic bottle, and some bandages.

As he got to work, Jade smiled up at him weakly. "Thank you for helping us. I can't believe you would risk your lives for us like that."

Chris fixed a pillow behind her head, then stroked the side of her face. "You're a strong one," he said, gazing down at her. "You will survive this. I feel it deep inside."

Standing at the end of the bed, Tiffany's stomach lurched as several different emotions ran through her, ranging from anger to jealousy. Was she about to be ignored again? Controlling her emotions, she walked up to the top of the bed and stood beside Chris. She rested a hand lightly on his shoulder and smiled down at Jade. "I feel it too, Jade. Be strong. Everything is going to work out just fine."

CHAPTER 25

Six Months Prior to the vPox Pandemic

Tomasso's Steakhouse was located in the Bella Vista neighborhood of South Philadelphia. It had an old-school prohibition-era feel to it. The tables were covered with crisp linen, the chairs upholstered in leather, and the mahogany-paneled walls were adorned with 1930s black and white photographs. If Kohler took a closer look, he was sure he would recognize a famous face or two.

He sat alone at a table, wearing a navy blue Madison blazer, a fitted white collared shirt, and gray chinos, no tie. On the plate in front of him was a mozzarella and tomato appetizer, while in the kitchen, a dry-aged porterhouse steak was being prepared for him on the hickory grill.

He took a sip from his mineral water and looked discreetly over at the bar, where Joey "The Horse" Borgano sat slouched on a stool nursing a whiskey. His FBI dossier stated he'd got the nickname by once imitating a certain scene from *The Godfather* involving a horse's head. Short, fat, with a mottled, olive-skinned complexion, he looked the typical mobster. He sounded like one too. Kohler could hear his coarse laughter from where he sat.

Standing to either side of Borgano were three of his crew, while at a table by the entrance sat two more. Heavyset, with thick mops of black hair and tight-fitting suits, Kohler had clocked them right away.

Borgano was a prominent *capo* in a Philadelphia crime family known as the South Philly Mob. As well as engaging in traditional mobster activities such as racketeering, extortion, and loansharking, the outfit was also heavily involved in the narcotics trade. Having flown into Philadelphia the previous day, it was for this aspect of the business that Borgano was at the top of Kohler's shortlist.

Halfway through his main course, he got the opportunity he was waiting for. From the corner of his eye, he spotted Borgano slide off his stool and head over to the far corner of the restaurant, where the restrooms were located. Kohler waited a few moments, then stood up and followed him over.

Before he reached the door, a squat man dressed in a sharkskin suit peeled off a nearby wall and blocked his way. "Bathroom is full," he told him in a polite but firm voice. "Come back in a few minutes."

"I'll wait," Kohler replied, and moved to stand over at the far side of the doorway.

The bull shook his head. "Go back to your table." His voice had lost its initial politeness.

Kohler was about to reply when the bathroom door opened and Borgano stepped out.

Before the bull could react, Kohler addressed him in a low-toned voice. "Mr. Borgano, may I have a word with you? I have something of interest to tell you."

Borgano glared at the bull, then at Kohler. "Why the hell would I want to talk to you?" he asked in a thick, rasping voice that had Sicilian written all over it from the moment he hit the first vowel.

"I have an interesting proposition for you. One that will make you and your associates very wealthy." Kohler looked around the room. While the most recent FBI report he'd read stated the steakhouse wasn't currently under surveillance, he wanted to keep his initial exposure as brief as possible.

Fortunately, so did Borgano. Eying him up and down, the *capo* made up his mind. He nodded to the bull. "Take him to the office and check him out." Without another word, he headed back to the bar.

The bull gestured for another of his associates to come over. Moments later, the two escorted Kohler down a narrow hallway that led to the back of the restaurant. At the end was a sturdy oak door that looked like it had been made when the building was first constructed. Fishing a key out of his pocket, the bull opened it, reached a hand around to switch on the light, and ushered Kohler inside.

Kohler stepped through the doorway to find himself in a medium-sized room that looked like it had once been used as a storeroom. At the center was an old wooden desk with a steel chair set to either side of it. In the far corner, a securely bolted door led out onto the street. Behind it, Kohler could hear the distant hum of traffic.

The bull took him over to the table. "Take off your shoes," he instructed him.

Kohler did as he was told. As soon as he was done, the second bull frisked him thoroughly, taking out his iPhone and wallet, and placing them on the table.

As he worked, the sharkskin-suited bull withdrew a small handheld object from one of the desk drawers. Kohler immediately recognized it. It was a bug detector, designed to pick up any signal emanating from a Bluetooth, Wi-Fi, GSM, or RF device. FBI-planted bugs had been the downfall of many a gangster, including the infamous "Dapper Don", John Gotti. Borgano wasn't taking any chances.

Once he'd given Kohler a full sweep that included his shoes and the items on the desk, the bull pulled out his own phone. He punched a key and placed it up to his ear. "He's clean, boss." He listened a while longer, then ended the call.

"Sit down and put on your shoes. Mr Borgano will be with you shortly."

Kohler sat down at the nearest chair and laced up his shoes. Straightening up, he reached a hand over to retrieve his wallet and phone.

The bull shook his head. "You'll get them back after your talk."

Kohler nodded, then sat back and waited. A smartphone made for a good eavesdropping device too.

Five minutes later, there was a rap on the back door. The bull went over, pulled back the bolt, and gestured to Kohler.

Kohler stood and walked over. Brushing past the man, he stepped out into a narrow alleyway, where the cloying smell of rotting food instantly assailed his senses. Lined up on either side of the alleyway were several trashcans stuffed to the brim with garbage bags.

A third crew member stood waiting for him. He took Kohler by the arm and escorted him to a black Lincoln Navigator parked at the end of the alley, its engine running. When they reached it, the bull opened the rear door. "Get in."

Kohler climbed inside the huge SUV and sat down. The door closed behind him, and the vehicle took off.

In the far seat, a lit cigar held between his short stubby fingers, Joey Borgano stared at Kohler through a set of hard eyes as black as coals. The FBI reports stated that the *capo* was suspected of killing over a dozen rival gang members. Up close, exuding a palpable air of menace, Kohler didn't doubt it for a moment.

"I told Carlo to circle the block," Borgano said in his grating voice. "By the time we get back, you need to have something good for me. Otherwise, I'm going to turf you out on the street. Carlo won't be slowing down while I do it neither. I don't like people wasting my time."

Kohler held his gaze. "It won't come to that," he said calmly. "You're going to be very interested in what I have to tell you."

One of Borgano's heavily-lidded eyes raised a fraction. "Before we get to that, I need to know who you are. You don't look like no ordinary cop on the make. You're too clean for that." The mobster flicked a speck of ash off his jacket. "And you're no wiseguy either, which raises the question, how do you know who I am? And how did you know where to find me?"

"Everything I know about you, I studied in your FBI dossier. It makes quite some reading."

A scowl came over Borgano's face. "You're a Fed? Get the fuck out of here. I got nothing to say to you. Carlo—"

"I'm no Fed, I'm a US Army intelligence officer," Kohler cut in, keeping his voice level. "With clearance to access FBI files plus any other three-lettered agency you care to name. Tracking you down was easy."

Borgano stared at him. "The Army? What does the Army want with a guy like me?"

"Nothing. I've sought you out in a private capacity." The Lincoln slowed down as it turned the block. Two hundred yards away, Kohler could make out the entrance to Tomasso's. "You may be interested to hear that I'm currently stationed in Colombia. I provide tactical intel on the drug cartels for the DEA and local law enforcement. Frankly, it's starting to tire me. Lately, I've been working on a new direction I'd like to take my career. One that intersects nicely with your line of business."

Borgano stared at him for several moments, then leaned forward and tapped Carlo on the shoulder, gesturing for him to continue driving. "All right. Just how exactly might we 'intersect'?" he asked, studying Kohler intently.

"How about at a destination of your choosing, where I will deliver you two hundred kilos of high-grade cocaine straight out of the factory? Does that sound like a good offer?"

Borgano showed no reaction, then slowly, the slightest trace of a smile appeared on his lips. "It beats waking up next to a horse's head. All right, Mister Lieutenant Army guy. You got my attention. Tell me more about this offer of yours."

CHAPTER 26

It was evening time, and Tiffany was preparing supper. She squatted beside the fire pit, its coals glowing beneath the grill, and used a wooden spoon to stir pasta around a pot of boiling water. Earlier, while Chris got the fire started, she'd taken the pot down to the river and filled it, then poured in ten drops of bleach as per his instructions. After letting the water stand for thirty minutes, she'd brought it to a boil, added salt, then thrown in two packages of spaghetti from her own dwindling supplies.

Next to the spaghetti, the contents from a can of diced tomatoes simmered in a smaller pot. She took out a sachet of garlic powder from her food bag and tipped out a generous amount. Stirring it in, she gazed up into the hills, where the last sliver of a deep orange sun dipped over the ridge line. As the valley slowly became engulfed in shadows, a thin smile came to her lips. With Jade incapacitated, and Karl Higgs subdued since his cowardly inaction back at their previous camp, she sensed the opportunity to assert herself within the group. Perhaps she had gotten a second chance after all.

This time, she was determined to make herself as useful as possible. She very much doubted Chris was the sort to tolerate a "spoiled, useless bitch." However, that didn't mean she had to throw out everything she'd previously learned in life, particularly where it came to men. She just needed to change her tactics, that was all.

Out of the corner of her eye, she spotted Higgs and Cornel approaching. For the past thirty minutes, the two had sat outside their tents, pitched to one side of the camp, and talked in low, urgent voices. Higgs had been the more animated of the two. It was plain to see he was unhappy with the current situation.

He hurried over to her ahead of Cornel, looking anxiously around him. "Tiffany, those two are total nut jobs," he said as soon as he reached her. "We need to get out of here before they shave our heads and we look as wacky as they do."

"They may be wacky, but, unlike you, they didn't behave like cowards today," Tiffany told him icily. She glanced at Cornel, and tried to read his expression. So far, he hadn't given any indication on how he felt about their situation. She guessed that like her, he realized they were safer with Chris and Mark than on their own. The events of that afternoon had clearly shown that.

"That's not fair! They had the element of surprise," Higgs protested. "By the time I knew what was happening, it was too late to do anything."

Tiffany snorted. "You behaved like a scared little rabbit today. If you'd picked your rifle up right away, maybe things would have turned out different." Turning her back on him, she crouched down in front of the fire and began stirring the sauce around in the pot again.

"Fine, stay here," Higgs said angrily. "Me and Cornel will go off without you. See how the whack jobs treat you then." With that, he stomped off in the direction of his tent.

"Don't worry," Cornel murmured before turning away to follow him. "I don't plan on going anywhere."

As she watched him leave, Tiffany smiled to herself. Though quiet and unassuming, Cornel was clearly the thinker in the group. She could see it in his eyes.

A few minutes later, Chris arrived, returning from the back of the camp where he'd disappeared to for the last twenty minutes. He carried a plastic tray, upon which a dozen steaks were neatly laid out.

"Is that venison?" Tiffany asked. She knew there were plenty of whitetail in the Cohutta. It was one of the reasons the group had chosen to come to the area.

"Boar," Chris replied.

"Boar?"

"Yes. Feral hog."

Tiffany resisted turning up her nose. Feral hog didn't sound very appetizing. Nonetheless, the meat looked good. Moist and thick, the ruby-colored steaks hardly had any fat on them. It had been over two weeks since she'd last eaten fresh meat.

"They look fantastic," she said, smiling at him.

Chris looked pleased. "I cut the meat from the haunch of a back leg. It's the best part of the animal for making steaks."

"Wonderful. Can I help you cook them?"

Chris put the tray down and walked over to the hut that served as the larder. He came back with a pepper mill and bag of sea salt. He handed them to Tiffany. "Season them, then put them on the grill."

Tiffany reached across and pulled the tray closer to her. Hunched over it, she began rubbing salt and pepper onto both sides of each steak.

While she worked, Chris stood to one side of her. Tiffany could sense him observing her closely. She knew why, too. When she'd gone down to the river earlier, she'd taken the opportunity to bathe. The water had been deliciously cool. As well as soaping her entire body, she'd washed her hair. Afterward, she brushed it out and changed into a fresh, tight-fitting T-shirt, cut-off jeans, and running shoes. Though she wore no makeup, she knew she looked good. Given the times, *real good*.

Once the steaks were prepared, she placed them on the middle of the grill, where the heat was the strongest. She looked up at Chris and smiled. "It's okay, I'll call you when everything is ready."

"Good," Chris said curtly, though Tiffany was pleased to detect a softer undertone beneath the gruff reply.

Nobody spoke much during dinner, and a palpable tension hung over the group. Sitting in a circle around the fire pit, Tiffany was the most relaxed. She chatted with Chris and Mark, finding out more about their lives. As usual, Cornel was the quietest, and ate his food meditatively, while Higgs glanced at her from time to time with a puzzled expression. She detected a hint of defeat in him. He was no longer in charge, and he knew it. Chris was, and that was where Tiffany focused her attention. She sat opposite him, her long legs stretched out to one side of the fire pit, her freshly-washed hair blowing gently in the evening breeze.

She learned that Chris had been the leader of a group who'd traveled to the Cohutta from Knoxville. They had lived at a place called Wasson Lodge until their camp was attacked a few nights after their arrival. That was when Chris had been shot and his people murdered.

At that point, Tiffany became a little confused. Chris declared that someone named Walter had betrayed him. Mark gently interrupted him to say that it had been a guy called Mason who'd attacked them, that it had nothing to do with Walter. The comment made Chris angry and he refused to accept it.

"Either way, thank God you survived," Tiffany said soothingly. "And Mark, it was so brave of you to save Chris that night. It would have been so much easier to just run away."

Mark smiled shyly. "I don't know what came over me. I saw them drag Chris and the others into the forest. Something inside me told me to go over and see if anyone was still alive. When I got there, I heard Chris moan, so I picked him up and took him to safety." He paused a moment as his emotions got the better of him. "I-I wasn't sure if he'd ever wake up. It took eight long days."

Tiffany shook her head in amazement. "*Something* told you to go over to him. That's so powerful. Like it was meant to happen."

Chris looked at her approvingly. "Yes, you understand."

As soon as dinner was over, Tiffany got up to check on Jade. Earlier, she'd taken in a plate of food for her. Now Jade was fast asleep, her empty plate lying beside the bed. Tiffany knelt down and picked it up.

The sound of rattling cutlery woke Jade up. "Who's that?" she asked sleepily. Recognizing who it was, her mouth turned down dismissively. "Oh…it's you."

Jade's attitude set Tiffany off. She couldn't help it. "Yes, just me," she hissed. "The one everyone's been laughing at. Well no one is laughing now. Dan is dead, and Karl is a proven coward. As for you? You're not doing that great either, are you?"

Jade shrank back, surprised by the ferocity of her tone. "Look, Tiffany, I'm sorry we've been mean to you, we shouldn't have behaved like that. But it was your own fault too. You behaved like such a…a…"

"A *princess*? You're right, I didn't deal with things well. The rest of you adjusted to the world after vPox far quicker than me. I tried to change, really I did. But you and Karl never gave me a chance. Cornel was the only one who was ever nice to me." Tiffany's gaze grew fiercer. "Everything is different now. Chris is running the show, so you better get used to it."

Before Jade could reply, she stood up and strode out of the tent, controlling her emotions as she returned to her place. It was pitch dark now, and she could barely make out anyone's faces. Judging from the uncomfortable silence, there hadn't been much in the way of conversation while she'd been away.

"You'll be pleased to hear that Jade ate all her dinner and is doing just fine," she said cheerfully. She looked around the circle. "Well, now. Did I miss anything?"

Ignoring her, Chris stood up and used a stick to drag the metal grill off the fire pit. He placed several more logs on, larger ones this time, and doused them with kerosene. With a *whoosh*, the wood crackled loudly, and the flames rose high enough for Tiffany to make out everybody's faces again.

She waited for Chris to sit back down, then turned her attention on him once more. "Today, you told me some interesting things about your plans for the tribe. I'm curious to hear more."

Sitting next to her, she sensed Higgs stiffen. "Cut that out, Tiffany," he muttered under his breath.

"What's there to tell?" Chris replied. "The old world is dead and gone, now a new one has taken its place. One without government or law. To survive, ordinary people need a strong leader. One who knows what it takes to survive."

"Someone like you, you mean?"

Chris nodded. "It is time for warriors to rule the Earth again. I will keep you safe, just as I did today." He stared through the flames at Tiffany. "You are part of my tribe now." He held a hand out to Higgs and Cornel. "All of you."

A look of alarm came over Higgs's face. "Look, Chris, we're all grateful for your help, but we're not looking to join your...your *tribe*."

Chris looked at him disdainfully. "I saw how you acted today. You are no leader."

"Either way, tomorrow we're leaving. Right, Cornel?"

Cornel stared into the fire, his head rigid. He said nothing.

"What about poor Jade?" Tiffany asked. "She's not ready to go yet. You plan on just leaving her here?"

For the first time since that afternoon, Higgs reverted to his former self. "You hypocritical bitch!" he snapped.

"What the fuck do you care about Jade? The two of you can't stand each other."

"Shut up!" Chris snapped, glowering at him. "Of course she cares. She's the only one of you three helping Jade. You think I don't see that?"

Higgs looked like he was about to say something, then checked himself. He glanced uncertainly at Cornel, who continued to stare into the flames.

A strange look came over Chris's face. "Mark, fetch me the medicine bag," he ordered.

"Uh...sure." Mark stood up and walked over to the tent. Moments later, he returned carrying the jute bag Chris had used earlier while treating Jade, and handed it to him.

Chris rummaged around the bag and drew out a scissors, a small hand mirror, and a pack of disposable razors.

He stared at the three. "Which of you will be the first to join me? Who is ready to become a true warrior?" His eyes bored into Tiffany's, the intensity of his gaze almost too hard to bear.

Deep within her, Tiffany felt a powerful emotion pull at her like a magnet. Ever since joining the group, she'd been scorned and ridiculed. Powerless to reply, her sense of isolation had grown each day. Now, that dynamic had changed. She felt stronger. *In control again.* But soon Jade would recover, then she and Higgs would resume their torment of her. To decisively change things required action on her part.

Scarcely able to believe what she was doing, she rose to her feet.

"*Tiffany!*" Higgs whispered in a pleading voice. "*Don't...*"

Tiffany ignored him. As if in a trance, she walked around the fire pit and stood in front of Chris. "I'm ready," she said in a clear, firm voice. "Do it."

Chris pointed to his feet. "Kneel."

Tiffany lowered herself onto her knees and bowed her head.

As Chris began cutting her hair, and her long, blonde locks fluttered to the ground around her, a thought entered her head. *The old world is dead and gone, now a new one has taken its place.*

CHAPTER 27

Six Months Prior to the vPox Pandemic

Rodadero Beach was situated five miles south of Santa Marta. Its large, crescent-shaped bay was perfectly suited to the high-rise, Miami-styled hotels along its palm-lined seafront, and it was one of the country's major tourist destinations. The only disappointment was the brown sand. As part of his brief as an intelligence officer, Kohler had visited the Darien Gap where the majority of cocaine shipments destined for the US were transported overland to Mexico. There, the beaches were pure white, and the sea an azure blue. Nevertheless, Kohler wasn't here for the view. Rodadero was safe, even by American standards, and, carrying a quarter of a million dollars in his suitcase, that was the most important thing right now.

He stood at the balcony of his Best Western hotel room and stared down fifteen floors to the beach below. It was *puente*, a holiday weekend, and the beach was packed with holidaymakers. Young children splashed about by the water's edge, while groups of men kicked a football around, or frolicked in the surf with their women. Attired in revealing bikini tops and thong bottoms, the women left little to the imagination.

Kohler had arrived in Santa Marta the previous evening. From the airport, he'd taken a taxi straight to the hotel, and on arrival had casually but firmly refused the bellboy's offer to carry his case. Shown to his room, he'd tipped the man with a five dollar note and ushered him out.

At 9 p.m., he'd ordered a chicken club sandwich and a Diet Coke. When it arrived, he pulled a chair out onto the balcony and ate his sandwich, staring down at the beach. The boardwalk had been busy. Street hawkers lined the pavement, selling barbecued food, cheap trinkets, and T-shirts, to remind Colombians of what a great holiday they'd had. Same as at every other beach resort Kohler had ever been to.

At 10 p.m., he'd gotten the call from Tony Mackenzie on his "clean phone." The DEA agent told him to expect to be collected by Juancho's men sometime the following morning, and taken to La Guajira. Afterward, he'd watched cable TV for a couple of hours, then gone to bed. That morning, he'd risen early, showered and packed, then ordered breakfast. It was now 10:50 a.m., and he'd been ready to leave for over three hours. The long wait had given him plenty of time to think.

He'd arrived back from Philadelphia over a week ago, where his series of meetings with Joey Borgano had gone well, and he'd left the city with a briefcase stuffed with cash. Five hundred thousand dollars to purchase two hundred kilos of cocaine, plus another fifty thousand to pay off the other participants in the operation, such as the Colombian base guards and the US ground crew at both the Tolemaida and Fort Bliss airbases.

Neither Kohler nor Mackenzie would get their cut until after the shipment had been delivered to Borgano. Then Kohler would be paid half a million dollars. Three hundred and fifty thousand would go to him, the remaining one hundred and fifty thousand to Mackenzie—which in Kohler's opinion was a lot of money for no more than a few phone calls on the DEA agent's part. Lacking personal contacts with the cartels, however, Kohler had no choice. That would soon change. All going well with Juancho, there was no reason why he couldn't arrange the next deal directly with the drug lord and keep the extra hundred and fifty thousand for himself. Kohler had no doubt he would be paid. The operation could be repeated several times a year, and would be hugely profitable to the crime family. While confident in his plan, Kohler intended on retiring once he'd accumulated a million dollars. Nothing was entirely without risk, though, and the longer the operation continued, the higher the chances were it would be eventually uncovered. Three runs and he was out. Borgano wouldn't be happy, Kohler knew that, and he needed to come up with the right excuse. That was what was going through his mind at that moment.

The phone rang, breaking him from his reverie. Stepping away from the balcony, he walked back into the room and picked it up off the wall. "Yes?"

"Senor Kohler, this is the front desk," a woman's voice said with an American-tinged accent. *"There are two gentlemen in the lobby who wish to see you. A Senor Lopez, and a Senor Rodriguez."*

"Send them up to my room," Kohler told her. "I'm expecting them."

"Right away, sir." The phone clicked dead and Kohler rested it back in its cradle.

Though a little tense, he felt no fear. Fear was an emotion he rarely experienced, though one he'd learned to expertly gauge in others, a trait he curiously shared with *El Patron*. Pablo Escobar had been a supremely confident person who, even under extreme pressure, never panicked or lost his head. Kohler just hoped he didn't suffer the same fate as the notorious drug trafficker, gunned down by DEA agents and Colombian police on the rooftop of a Medellin apartment block.

A few minutes later, there was a soft rap on the door. Kohler crossed the room and opened it.

There was nothing subtle about the two men who stood in the hallway. Kohler would have recognized them as typical *mafiosos* if he'd passed them on the street. Around five-ten, swarthy, and heavyset, both had the physical muscularity of bulls. They wore designer jeans, Lacoste polos—one yellow, one pink—and plenty of gold. Kohler immediately took them for brothers, despite the different *appelidos* they had given at the desk.

"Don Max?" asked the one wearing pink, the slightly larger of the two. "I'm Benjie Orejuela. This is my brother, Fernie. May we come in?"

Kohler opened the door wider for them. "Of course."

The two brothers filed into the room. Kohler closed the door after them and took them over to the table. He indicated that they sit down.

Fernie shook his head politely. "We need to leave now," he said, speaking in the same heavily-accented English as his brother. "We have a long drive ahead of us."

He looked over to where Kohler had left his suitcase at the side of the bed. Hidden underneath a spare set of clothes was a quarter of a million dollars in $50- and $100-dollar bills. "May I help you with your things?"

Kohler hesitated a moment, then nodded. It seemed senseless to object. Soon he would be riding through the barren Guajira Desert, at the mercy of these men.

Fernie strode over to the bed and picked up the case. At the small of his back, Kohler could make out the bulge of a pistol tucked into its paddle holster underneath his shirt.

"Let's go," the *mafioso* said, straightening up. A minute later, the three were at the elevator, where Benjie and Fernie maintained a wary presence while they waited for the elevator to arrive.

Down in the lobby, the brothers stood to one side of the counter while Kohler checked out, then all three strode out of the building and into the morning sunshine.

At the bottom of the steps, a black Ford Explorer with tinted windows was waiting. A man, about ten years older than the brothers, with clipped salt and pepper hair, jumped out of the driver's door. As soon as Kohler reached him, he opened the back door and Kohler climbed inside.

Fernie got in next, carrying the case, while Benjie walked around to the far side and got in the front passenger door. As soon as he'd closed it, he picked up a semi-automatic rifle whose stock had been resting in the footwell, its muzzle facing toward the roof.

The driver spoke rapid Spanish into a two-way radio, then stepped on the pedal. As they took off, a white Toyota Frontier fifty yards ahead moved smoothly away from the curb. Though he didn't look around, Kohler was sure a similar vehicle had likewise slipped out onto the street behind them.

He sat back in his seat and exhaled slowly. It would take five hours to reach La Guajira. There was a lot of empty desert on the way. Perfect for dumping bodies. If he made it to his destination, he was confident he would return to Tolemeida in one piece.

CHAPTER 28

With a frown of concentration etched on his brow, Chris applied the final touches to what remained of Tiffany's hair. Though he'd given her the tiny hand mirror earlier, she hadn't dared look at herself yet. She would wait until later, when she was alone.

At last, Chris put away the bottle of peroxide, stood up, and lifted her to her feet. He brought her closer to the fire, and gazed at his work. "You look good," he grunted appreciatively. "Fit to stand beside your chief."

Tiffany took that as her cue. She stared down at Higgs and Cornel, who both still sat by the fire pit, and smiled pleasantly at them. "It's been a long day for everyone. I think we should all go to bed, don't you?"

Neither of the two said anything. Just like when they'd come under attack that day, Cornel wore an inscrutable air that gave nothing away. The expression on Higgs's face, however, told her precisely what was on his mind. Pure horror.

Glancing briefly at Chris, Tiffany linked her arm in his, and the two headed in the direction of his tent. Behind her, she heard Higgs whispering furiously. She didn't care. So long as Cornel stayed on, she was sure he would still be there the following day. Higgs didn't have the guts to go anywhere on his own.

Inside the tent, Chris lit a kerosene lamp and a warm amber glow illuminated the room. Tiffany moved in closer to him and murmured in his ear. "We need some privacy, don't you think?" She pointed to the far corner of the room where Jade was fast asleep. "I won't feel comfortable with you if she's here."

With a curt nod, Chris placed the lamp down on the tree stump and walked over to where Jade's belongings had been stacked against the wall. He picked them up and, without a word, walked out of the tent. A moment later, Tiffany heard him call out to Mark to help him set up her tent.

She knelt down by the lamp and raised the hand mirror to her face. Adjusting the angle, she let out a short gasp when she caught sight of her shorn scalp, with its ridge of spiky bleached hair running down the middle. Taking a deep breath, she examined her new hair style from a different angle. Though severe, there was something *sexy* about it, she thought to herself...something—

"Tiffany?" Jade called out from her bed. "Is that you?"

Tiffany spun around to see Jade craning her neck forward with a confused look. She picked up the lantern and walked over to her.

"Yes, it's me. The *new* me," she said, squatting beside Jade so that she could see her better. "What do you think?"

Jade sat up in the bed in shock. "My God, Tiffany! What have you done?"

"What's wrong? Don't you like it?"

Jade looked at her, aghast. "Are you crazy? Of course I don't."

Tiffany shrugged. "Well, Chris likes it, and that's all that counts. Oh, speaking of which, he's outside preparing your new accommodation."

"What do you mean?"

"You'll be back in your tent tonight. It's for your sake as much as mine. It would be kind of *pervy* for you to watch me and him…you know…"

Jade had recovered her composure by now. "I've no intention of staying here with you two," she said stiffly. "You do realize you've gone totally insane, don't you?

Tiffany shook her head. "No, Jade, it's the world that's gone insane. I'm just dealing with the new reality." She smiled mockingly. "I thought you'd be proud of how I'm coping. There hasn't been a complaint from me all evening."

"What does Karl make of this?" Jade asked, ignoring her remark.

"Karl the coward? He's urging Cornel to leave with him tomorrow. I told him you weren't fit to go yet, but he didn't seem to care."

Jade gritted her teeth. "I'll be ready. Don't you worry about that."

Tiffany smiled. "No need to hurry. Cornel has no intentions of leaving, and I very much doubt Karl will go by himself. Or worse still, with somebody who can barely walk by her—"

She broke off when Mark entered the tent. He came over to the two and stared down at Jade. "Ready?"

"Oh, I'm ready," Jade replied. "Please. Get me out of here."

Mark bent over and bundled the diminutive Jade easily into his arms, then stood up and walked over to the entrance.

As soon as they'd left, Tiffany thought hard. Once fit, no doubt Jade would urge Higgs to leave the camp, perhaps Cornel might even go too. The thought of remaining alone with Chris and Mark sent a shiver down her spine, and for a moment she wondered if she'd made the right decision.

She gathered her resolve and ran through the next step of her plan. If everything worked out the way she hoped, soon Jade wouldn't be in position to leave the camp for quite a while. The thought of what she had in store for her put a smile on Tiffany's face. Perhaps Jade was right. Perhaps she'd gone insane after all.

CHAPTER 29

Six Months Prior to the vPox Pandemic

The three-vehicle convoy traveled all day. First north, along the Caribbean coast, where each town they passed through consisted of no more than a few scruffy buildings set on either side of the highway. The sea was an inviting blue, though, and the unending stretches of beach were as white as those Kohler had seen in the Darien. Set along the beach front was the occasional brightly-painted shack advertising yoga or surf lessons. Kohler even spotted an odd *gringo* or two.

At Riohacha, the vehicles turned east and headed inland toward Maicao, a notorious smuggler's town a few miles from the Venezuelan border. Nobody talked much. Dozing off and on, Kohler sat in the back seat of the Explorer, staring out at the scorched, barren landscape flashing by. Once away from the sea, the Guajira terrain took on a more somber tone, threatening, even.

An hour later, twenty kilometers from Maicao, they turned south and headed down a badly-paved road into an area of semi-desert scrubland and hilly terrain, arriving at the outskirts of a dusty little town still baking in the late afternoon heat. The Explorer slowed, then pulled up outside a roadside cafe, though neither the lead Toyota nor the trailing vehicle stopped. Both continued south. To pick up Juancho, Kohler presumed.

Fernie, who had been asleep for most of the journey, nudged Kohler in the ribs. He pointed out the window. "*A comer,*" he said. "Let's eat."

Kohler got out of the car, and a wave of heat swept over him like an oven door had just opened. He couldn't imagine what the drive must have been like in the days before air-conditioning.

The three walked over to the restaurant. Like so many buildings in the region, it was made of no more than bare cinderblock and wood, though on one side it had a newly-built veranda, and that was where the brothers took him.

Benjie greeted the *dueno* familiarly, then sat down at a table below a ceiling fan and ordered food for the three. Kohler was famished. He hadn't eaten since breakfast, and was thankful when, a few minutes later, a large bowl of stew was placed on the table in front of them. Given the speed with which it arrived, he guessed that the restaurant owner had been expecting them.

Benjie poured out a generous serving into a terracotta bowl. "This is *sancocho,*" he told him. "Traditional Colombian soup made of chicken and vegetables." He patted Kohler on the back. "Eat up. *Es muy sabroso.*"

Kohler didn't normally eat Colombian cuisine. Servicemen at the base generally didn't. Served with rice, avocado, and *aji picante* on the side, he had to admit the broth was exquisite. Kohler had an excellent palate, and could taste the delicate flavors of cumin and fresh cilantro coming through. "It's excellent," he said, wolfing down another spoonful.

"What did I tell you?" Benjie said, looking pleased. "I don't understand why you *gringos* come here and eat all that shitty American food." He patted his not-insubstantial belly, then flexed an even more substantial bicep. "See? Colombian food makes you *fuerte!*"

"I don't doubt it," Kohler murmured politely. "Tell me, when do I get to meet Juancho?"

"He'll be here soon. He didn't bring you all the way here for nothing." Benjie grinned, exhibiting a set of perfect white teeth, other than a gold-capped one at the front. "That would be rude."

When they finished eating, the proprietor took away the empty plates and returned shortly with a dessert of freshly sliced mango, papaya, and pineapple. Benjie ordered coffee, and soon Kohler was sipping a brewed coffee far superior to what he'd drunk at the Best Western that morning.

A thought occurred to him. "Benjie, does Juancho own this place?"

"Why do you ask?"

"Because the food is too good for any ordinary roadside shack. And if I'm not mistaken, this coffee was made for export, not domestic use."

The *mafioso*'s smile grew larger, revealing another gold tooth at the side of his mouth. "You are very clever, Max. Good. My *jefe* likes clever people. This is a dangerous profession we have chosen, and gets harder every year. To survive, you must be smart." He pointed out at the highway. "Did you know that in the old days, this road used to be turned into an airstrip at nights? DC3s landed here. They loaded up with as many kilos as their cargo bays could hold, then flew all the way up to the US." He sighed and shook his head. "Radar detection is too advanced these days. Everything is smuggled overland via *El Darien* up to Mexico."

Kohler nodded. "Before cocaine, they used to load bales of marijuana onto the planes, and fly up to Miami on the 73rd Meridian flight route. Cocaine is a far more profitable haul, though."

Benjie grinned. "You know our history. *Muy bien, parcero.* Juancho will respect that." He gazed south along the highway, barely visible in the gathering dusk. It was 5:45 p.m., and night fell early this close to the Equator. "If I'm not mistaken, here he comes now."

Kohler spotted the headlights from two vehicles driving down the side of a nearby hill. When the first one reached the bottom, it turned onto the highway and approached them at speed.

Kohler saw that it was the white Toyota Frontier returning. When it reached them, rather than stopping outside, it drove around to the back of the restaurant and out of sight. Moments later, there was the sound of doors banging, then a voice called out in a pleading, frightened tone. It cut off mid-stream with a short yelp.

Kohler glanced at Benjie and raised an eyebrow.

Benjie shrugged. "The owner, Javier. Sometimes he doesn't treat his staff so good."

The second vehicle arrived, a dark-silver Mercedes SUV. It pulled into the unpaved forecourt and parked alongside the Explorer, kicking up a cloud of dirt and sand in its wake.

As soon as it stopped, three men jumped out. One stepped around to the back passenger door and opened it. A man dressed in a black silk shirt, designer jeans, and tan Oxfords stepped out. In his late-fifties, he looked well-preserved, and shared the same bull-like physique as the Orejuela brothers. His hair was jet black, as was the well-trimmed goatee, though Kohler suspected both were dyed.

He strode across to the veranda, accompanied by his men. Before he reached them, the two brothers stood up. Kohler hesitated a moment, then did likewise.

The man stopped in front of Kohler. "Max? I am Juan Pablo," he said, taking Kohler's hand in a vice-like grip and shaking it hard. "My friends call me Juancho. Please, do the same."

Letting go of Max's hand, he ordered Benjie to bring him over a chair, then indicated to Kohler to sit down. Benjie returned with a chair from the next table, and the four sat down.

Making himself comfortable, Juancho pulled out a cheroot cigar from his top pocket and stuck it in his mouth.

From across the table, Fernie took out a lighter and reached an arm across to light it for him.

After a couple of puffs, Juancho leaned back and addressed Kohler in almost perfect English. "Max, my apologies for dragging you to such a miserable part of the world," he said in a tone that was anything but apologetic. "Perhaps Tony might have told you, I make a point of only doing business with men who I have first looked in the eye." He drew his chair in closer to Kohler's. "In our line of business, there is no greater issue than that of trust, no?"

Kohler felt the intensity of the drug lord's stare as his eyes bore into his. If Joey Borgano had a cold, ruthless aura, the Colombian ex-paramilitary's was twice as intimidating. Though smiling, his eyes were dark and menacing. From his study of the Northern Bloc of the AUC, Kohler knew how truly barbaric the paramilitaries had been. They'd controlled their territory around Santa Marta with an iron grip.

He stared back at Juancho, keeping his emotions under control. "I understand perfectly. It is important for me, too. Trust can only be truly gauged face-to-face." Kohler trusted this man about as much as he trusted a snake. Only the mutually beneficial business they were about to undertake gave him any confidence as to how this meeting would go down.

Juancho nodded appreciatively. "Thank you," he said, his gaze softening slightly. "Tony has told me all about you. He says you are the brains behind this operation. Is that true?"

Kohler shrugged. "I guess you could say that. I've put a lot of work into the planning."

"And such an ambitious plan, too. Tell me, are you're sure you can get the product safely into the US?"

"Very confident."

Juancho gazed at him keenly. "Two hundred kilos of pure grade cocaine is a lot to dispose of. You must have somebody big lined up to distribute it, no?"

Kohler hesitated, unsure how to reply. If possible, he would prefer not to reveal his connection with Borgano and the South Philly Mob. The less people knew, the better.

Sensing his reluctance, Juancho leaned back in his seat and waved a hand. "That's okay, it's only professional curiosity on my part." He winked at the Orejuela brothers. "Besides, I learned from Tony that you were in Philadelphia last week." He clicked his fingers. "Meeting what type of people did he say, Benjie?"

Benjie chuckled. "The pasta-eating variety, *Don Juancho*."

Juancho smiled, though his eyes remained as cold as ever. "Tell me, Max? Did you eat pasta while you were in Philadelphia?"

Kohler felt a surge of anger run through him. Mackenzie had revealed more than he ought to have. "As a matter of fact, I did," he replied evenly. "*Spaghetti alle vongole*, to be exact." Kohler's second meeting with Borgano had been at a small family restaurant just outside of the city. The food had been outstanding.

"Excellent. Did it match up to our Colombian fare?"

"Almost. Not quite."

Juancho clapped his hands and laughed, a thunderous guffaw that emanated from deep within his belly. "How very diplomatic of you, Max. I must say, you play your cards close to your chest. Not like Tony. A couple of drinks and a line of *perico*, and he talks like a woman. I can't get him to shut up."

At that moment, the proprietor came out with a cup of coffee and placed it on the table in front of Juancho, along with a small bowl of Muscovado sugar.

Juancho heaped in a spoon, then stirred his coffee. He took a short sip, and placed the cup back down on the table again. "Now, to business," he said briskly. "Fernando has counted the money. It's all present and correct. Next time we meet, you will bring me the second half. In return, I will supply you with two hundred kilos of the purest cocaine you will find in Colombia."

"Where will the meeting take place?" Kohler asked. He hoped it would be somewhere close to the Tolemeida airbase. The last thing he wanted to do was to transport the shipment from La Guajira. Mackenzie had assured him that wouldn't be the case.

"I own several *bodegas* in Bogota. There is one in the south city that should suit our purposes. Is that good for you?"

A warehouse in Bogota was ideal. It was under a three-hour drive to Melgar from there.

Kohler nodded. "Perfect."

"Good. I can arrange to have the product transported there next week." Juancho looked at Kohler inquiringly. "What day of the week will suit you?"

"Wednesday evening would be good."

"So be it. Wednesday evening it is." Juancho drained his cup, then stood up. "If you please, follow me, I have something to show you."

Kohler stood up, surprised when Juancho headed inside the restaurant instead of over to the SUV, where his men stood waiting. Leading the way, Juancho took him down a long corridor to the back of the building and into the last room at the end.

Kohler followed him in, then stopped in his tracks by the doorway.

Inside the room were four men, presumably those from the Toyota that had parked around the back earlier. Unlike either Juancho or the Orejuela brothers, none were well dressed, and wore ill-fitting jeans and grubby T-shirts. All four had the same hard-eyed expressions on their faces, though. Nonetheless, it was not them that caught Kohler's attention.

At the center of the otherwise bare room, a chair had been placed. On the chair, stripped to the waist, sat a man with a bruised and bloodied face. As Juancho strode over to him, he looked up, his eyes bulging with terror. "*Patron!*" he gasped. "*Por favor…perdoname.*"

Juancho beckoned to Kohler. "Come, Max. See what we do with *un raton* in my country."

Kohler stepped forward. When he got closer, he saw that the prisoner's hands had both been strapped to the armrests. Several of his fingernails had been pulled off, and they oozed with blood.

"There's no need to be alarmed," Juancho said as Kohler drew abreast of him. "You are not in any danger." His voice grew harsher. "On the other hand, this man you see before you is in great danger. In fact, his life is almost over."

"What did he do?" Kohler asked, keeping all emotion out of his voice.

"He betrayed my organization, and for that he will pay the ultimate price." Juancho leaned over and stroked the side of the man's face with the back of his hand. "Part of that price means that he will die knowing that both his wife and beautiful daughter will die very soon too. Though not before my men enjoy themselves with them first."

The man sobbed loudly. "I beg you, *Don Juancho!*" he said in Spanish. "Do what you want with me, but spare my family. They are innocent."

Juancho shook his head. "You know that cannot be, Enrique. When an *Urbano* betrays his fellow brothers, a strong message needs to be sent to all in the organization, so that they think long and hard before doing anything as foolish as you. Besides…" he added, "is your wife all that innocent? Did she not know twenty years ago that she was marrying a *sicario?* A paid killer who had no compunction in robbing other women of their families?"

Enrique's expression grew more pained. "Then my daughter. Spare her at least. I beseech you."

Juancho shook his head once more. "Sometimes the innocent must die. If anyone should know that, it is you." He nodded to one of his men, who stood behind the prisoner. "*Matalo*," he said.

The man withdrew a ten-inch knife from his pocket. Stepping forward, he grabbed Enrique's head and jerked it back. With a smooth motion, he sliced across his neck several times, cutting the carotid arteries and jugular veins. Enrique spluttered something incomprehensible, his eyes bulging even larger. With a final sweeping motion, his executioner thrust his head forward.

Enrique shuddered violently in his chair, gasping for air while his legs thrashed out in front of him. Kohler watched in fascination as blood poured down his chest and onto the dirt floor. He was an intelligence officer, not a field soldier, and had never seen a man die before. Today, he was witnessing it most graphically.

After a few more seconds, Enrique stopped thrashing other than for an occasional twitch as the last few seconds of his life came to an end. Then he slumped there, motionless, his head resting on his chest.

"Max, I brought you here today to witness how my organization deals with traitors," Juancho said. "You need to know that if you ever betray me, you will die in a similar fashion. Please, do not think you are immune to my reach once you return to the US. I have many associates there. Think of your family. Thanks to his selfishness, Enrique's family must suffer the consequences of his actions along with him."

Kohler was unmarried, both his parents were dead, and he had one brother in Tennga, Georgia he hadn't talked to in years. Nonetheless, he took the drug lord's point. "I would never dream of it," he said. "I'm not that crazy."

"Good." Juancho motioned to the executioner. The man stepped around the chair and lifted Enrique's head back, to reveal a bloody gash still dripping profusely. He squatted beside him and inserted his knife just below the jawline and began making another slit.

"What is he doing?" Kohler asked, transfixed by the man's actions.

"Raul is making Enrique a tie for his funeral," Juancho explained. "*La corbata*, we call it here. Perhaps you know it as the 'Colombian necktie.' Wait. You will see."

A few moments later, the executioner stood up again and Kohler had the opportunity to observe his work. Enrique's tongue had been pulled through the upper slit in his throat, its pink tip clear to see.

"Just like a tie, isn't it?" Juancho said softly. "But it's an urban myth that *La corbata* can kill a man in and of itself. That's why it needs to be applied post-mortem. Later tonight, he will be left in the village square for all to see how the *Urbanos* deal with traitors." He clapped Kohler on the back and ushered him back toward the door. "You must be tired after your day's travel. Tonight, I welcome you to my home, where my wife will cook you the most beautiful *Bandeja Paisa*. First thing in the morning, Benjie and Fernie will drive you back to Santa Marta."

Wordlessly, Kohler turned his back on Enrique, though his grotesquely disfigured corpse remained imprinted in his mind's eye for many more hours.

***

The following day, twenty minutes after being deposited at Santa Marta airport by the Orejuela brothers, Kohler received a call from Mackenzie.

"How was your trip?" the DEA agent inquired. *"Interesting?"*

"You could say that," Kohler replied acidly. "I learned how Colombian *mafiosos* deal with traitors in their organization."

Mackenzie chuckled loudly. *"La corbata Colombiana? Not a pretty way to die, is it? Don't worry, Juancho liked you. 'Ice cool' is how he described you. He just wanted you to know how he deals with anyone who dares to double-cross him, that's all."*

"So long as he delivers on Wednesday. That's all I care about."

"He will. Juancho built his reputation by playing things straight. Just concentrate on getting the product into the base, and over to the States. Stay focused."

"I'm always focused," Kohler said, then hung up.

As he boarded his flight back to Bogota, there was only one thing Kohler remained focused on: how, on his second run, he would deal directly with Juancho. No way in hell was he paying Mackenzie one hundred and fifty thousand dollars for zero risk and a few phone calls. Besides, the man was a liability.

CHAPTER 30

Jonah sat on the porch steps of Chickasaw, the cabin he'd hauled up from their old camp and single-handedly rebuilt. It was 9 p.m., and he was dog-tired after a long day's fishing. His shoulders slouched, and he held a customary can of beer in his hand, his third and last of the evening (though he might slip one more in if Colleen wasn't looking).

Above him, a wan moon limped slowly across the valley, peeking in and out of the clouds, and in the nearby forest, insects chirruped loudly. On top of the nearest hill, Jake Calley, a Benton man, was on watch, armed with a pair of Bushnell night-vision binoculars, and around both camps, a combined force of at least six guards patrolled the perimeters, providing security for all.

"Peace in the Valley," isn't that what that geezer Elvis once sang? Jonah thought to himself with a contented sigh. Despite his initial reservations, he was pleased to have come up to the Alaculsy Valley. The two camps were well-organized and battle-hardened since their confrontation with Mason, and Jonah felt the most secure he'd been since that first day he and Colleen had run into trouble in Orlando.

He'd made new friends too, such as Walter, Billy, and Clete, and his favorite pastime, fishing, was as good here as at the lake. Even better, perhaps. Just that morning, Clete had collected him and Billy and driven north out of the camp, saying nothing more other than that he had a treat in store for them.

He wasn't kidding. He took the two to a place known locally as the "Conassauga Snorkel Hole," a large pool of water about the size of a football pitch that positively teemed with fish. Clete proudly told them that over seventy species could be spotted there on any given day.

Donning snorkels and masks that the Tennessean provided for them - to Jonah and Billy's amazement - once underwater, it was like being in an aquarium. Freshwater drum swam in large schools in the deeper pools, while sporting fish such as bass and bream were abundant, and brightly-colored darters and shiners spawned in the shallows. The waters were also home to mussels, snails, crayfish, salamanders, and turtles. It had been a magical day, and after swimming for hours, the three returned home with their buckets full of stock for the pond.

Jonah took another slug from his beer and leaned back against the porch step. Suddenly, a few hundred yards farther north, a string of lights flickered, then remained on, illuminating the Eastwood front yard, where they kept their vehicles parked.

Jonah smiled. It had been two days since the waterwheel had been installed. It looked like Walter had found his transformer.

***

The following morning, he sought Walter out and found him in his workshop. Billy was there too. He held a pair of wire strippers and was busy removing the coating from the end of a length of electrical cable. Spotting Jonah arriving, he looked up from his work and smiled.

"Yer a busy little fella, aren't yeh?" Jonah greeted him. "If I was to hazard a guess, I'd say yeh had something to do with them lights I saw come on last night. Am I right?"

"He sure did," Walter said. "Couldn't have got them going without him."

"But no need for poor old Jonah though," the Irishman said with a pained expression. "Looks like I'm just the donkey around here when yeh need something hauled, while youse lot do all the cool stuff, that it?"

"Of course not!" Billy exclaimed, looking guilty. "When Walter asked me to help yesterday, you'd already gone home after our swim. Otherwise you could have helped too, honest."

Jonah ruffled his hair. "Well, that makes me feel better. So how about it? Yeh going to give me a gander how yis set everything up? I'm sure I'll understand *some* of it."

Billy set his tools down on the bench. "Come on, Walter. Let's show him!"

With Billy leading the way, the three walked through the garden and over to the farmhouse. They entered through the back door and through the kitchen into the hall. Halfway down was an old door painted a dull cream color. Walter pushed it open.

"This is the utility room. No one's used it since the Bentons stayed with us." He ushered Jonah inside. "It suits our needs perfectly."

The room measured about twelve feet by eight. It smelled dank and musty, and the paint on the walls was flaking off.

Walter pointed over to where a rectangular metal box sat on the floor at the far side. "That's the charge controller," he said, bringing Jonah across to it. "I stripped it out of an old camper, then fed a cable from the creek all the way here."

"Nice job." Jonah peered over to where, above the controller, a small plastic box was screwed to the wall. On it, an LED display read *13.3*. "Is that the voltage reading?" he asked.

Walter nodded. "It's a little low right now because the batteries aren't fully charged."

Jonah raised an eyebrow. "Batteries?" He looked around the room. "Where? I don't see them."

Billy strode across the room to where a large plastic container sat in one corner. Like a magician producing a rabbit out of a hat, he dramatically lifted it up to reveal a row of double-stacked car batteries underneath. There were six in total, hooked up to each other with electrical cables.

"Once I get the chance, I'm going to replace them with deep cycle batteries," Walter said. "They're better for a renewable energy source such as we're using."

Jonah raised an eyebrow. "Deep cycle batteries? Never heard of them."

"A car battery is designed to deliver short bursts of energy, like to start the engine," Billy broke in, anxious to show off his knowledge. "Deep cycle batteries are better for providing a steady, continuous rate."

Jonah stared at him. "Yer a regular little Einstein, aren't yeh? Watch out, Walter. In a couple of years, he'll have taken over yer job!"

"That's the plan," Walter replied. "We need to prep the next generation well so that they can take things to the next level."

Jonah chuckled. "Enough of that. I like the level we're at just fine. Then again, I'm a simple man with simple pleasures." He pointed to a nearby shelf, where there was another piece of electrical equipment - a blue and white plastic box. A cable from the top battery led up to it. "Duralast inverter…2000 watt," he read out. "What does this contraption do?"

"That converts the twelve-volt power from the battery to standard household power," Walter explained. He pointed over to a medium-sized chest freezer in the far corner of the room. "Things like that contraption there."

"And the house lights," Billy piped up.

Jonah scratched his head. "Who'd have thought those old pieces of deck wood we nailed together could generate enough power to keep all this going?" He rubbed his hands together. "So tell me this, and tell me no more: when are yeh going to get the lecky going over at our camp? Colleen will be thrilled to be able to read her Kindle at nights. The kerosene lamp she's using is woeful. Stinks up the cabin too."

"Soon," Walter promised. "I need to do some more load tests first. Worst case scenario, we can always build another waterwheel. It's not like we're short of materials."

Jonah threw up his hands in horror. "Not on yer Nelly! Yeh'll need to find someone else to do that again!"

Billy blinked hard, then caught himself. "I know you're joking," he said, looking up at the Irishman. "You can't fool me anymore."

Jonah grinned. "Who said I was joking? But look, if yeh can negotiate the double rate we were talking about the other day, then I'm game ball!"

CHAPTER 31

Six Months Prior to the vPox Pandemic

It was drizzling rain in the Candelaria, Bogota's historic center, where the Spanish had built their administrative capital almost five hundred years ago. Situated on a vast plateau at an elevation of eight and a half thousand feet, the rain came as no surprise, and Kohler wore a leather jacket, jeans, and boots as he walked down a narrow cobblestoned street in the evening gloom.

On his back he carried a worn daypack that looked like it might contain a spare set of clothes. However, if someone was to catch a glimpse of the Beretta M9 tucked inside the shoulder holster he wore underneath his jacket, they might suspect something different.

He entered a small plaza surrounded by squat buildings with terracotta roofs and graffiti-covered walls, most of it political in nature. All around the square were the city's main universities and, like anywhere else in the world, students liked to protest.

Kohler wondered about what, exactly. In Colombia, only the rich could afford third level education, the barrio dwellers and *campesinos* barely made it through high school. Increasingly, the *campesinos* were being forced off their land by paid killers—the likes of Juancho and his crew—so that the agribusinesses could grow palm oil on their rich, fertile soil. If a *campesino* refused, soon enough, a grenade would roll in through his front door. What was left of the family sold up quickly after that, then they too became barrio dwellers.

The palm oil was used to make biodiesel, and sold to Americans obsessed with renewable fuels. In the meantime, huge swaths of pristine hardwood forests were being destroyed, after being sold by Colombian politicians to friends of American ex-presidents at a tidy profit for all. The same ex-presidents who ostensibly believed in the environment and other worthy causes, so long as it didn't impinge on their own bottom line. Not that Kohler cared. The world was no place for the innocent or the unwary. Just ask Enrique's wife or daughter. One needed independent means to live well, and Kohler was hellbent on acquiring those means. He didn't give a damn how, either.

At the far corner of the square was a coffee shop. Kohler crossed over to it and stepped into a dimly-lit room with only a couple of low-watt bulbs hanging from the ceiling for illumination. He ordered a coffee, and sat down at a tiny metal table by the window, keeping the daypack on his back. Presently, the young lady came around the counter and served him his drink.

He heaped a spoonful of sugar into his cup, stirred it, and took a sip. The quality was mediocre. Most of Colombia's quality coffee was for export only, unless one went to a more upmarket establishment, such as a Juan Valdez coffee shop.

Kohler wasn't in Bogota for the coffee, though. He was waiting for word from Tony Mackenzie that would inform him of where he was to meet Juancho and pick up almost a quarter ton of high-grade cocaine with a US street value of over twenty million dollars. In his pocket, set to vibrate, he carried a cheap Nokia phone he'd purchased two days ago, along with a brand new sim card. Just like in Santa Marta, only Mackenzie had the number.

Once he'd picked up the product, he would drive back to the base in a hired car, where his two paid guards, Santiago and Carlos, were due to arrive on duty at 8 p.m. He'd hired the car that morning, a mid-sized SUV. It wasn't unusual for US servicemen to hire cars from time to time, and he'd previously done two dry runs. On both occasions, he'd simply shown his ID at the entrance gate and had been waved through. Paying off the guards was just an extra precaution.

While he waited, Kohler felt no sense of unease. He simply wasn't wired that way. Everything had been set in motion. Now he would execute his plan.

He was on his second coffee when the phone vibrated in his pocket. He reached into his jeans and pulled it out to see that a text message had arrived: *RV AT 20:00 HOURS. GAS STATION ON CORNER OF AVENIDA DE LAS AMERICAS & CARRERA 36. A WHITE HONDA CIVIC WILL BE WAITING FOR YOU. PLEASE CONFIRM.*

Kohler hit the Reply button, typed *MSG RECEIVED* on the tiny display, and pressed *Send*. Then he powered down the phone and put it back in his pocket.

He checked his watch. It was 6:45 p.m. The Las Americas district was in the south of the city, and traffic would still be heavy at this time of the evening. Gulping down the last of his coffee, he stood up, paid his bill at the counter, and left the cafe.

He'd left his hire car at a small parking lot a couple of blocks south of the square. Shoulders hunched against the rain, he walked down Carrera 4, past the Hotel El Dorado, its walls painted a hideous shade of green, and turned left onto Calle 12. A few yards up, he entered through the lot's steel gates, handed the young attendant his stub, and paid the fee.

Inside his vehicle, a Toyota Prado, he pulled out a detailed map of the city and found the cross street he was looking for. Carrera 36 was approximately a third of the way down Avenida de las Americas. Kohler had an excellent memory. He calculated his route, started the engine, and drove out of the lot.

Forty minutes later, he was driving down a busy four-lane highway amid thick traffic. Both sides of the Avenida were littered with bars, clubs, and eateries, and people thronged the streets. Ahead, buses and *collectivos* stopped constantly in front of him. Unlike in the US, they made unscheduled stops to either pick up or drop off passengers.

After driving under the Norte-Quito-Sur overpass, he moved into the outer lane, watching the street numbers as they flashed by. He passed Carrera 35 and immediately spotted the gas station looming ahead on the next corner. He slowed down and flipped on his indicator. Moments later, he pulled into the station.

At the far corner, a white Honda Civic sat parked with its lights off. Kohler drove over to it, the rain-slicked forecourt glistening under his headlights. Before he reached it, the Civic's lights came on and it drove out a side exit and onto a small street. Kohler followed at a discreet distance.

For the next thirty minutes, he drove through the back streets of South Bogota. Once off the main road, there was little in the way of street signs, and he was soon lost in the huge sprawling city. Finally, approaching a hilly area, the two vehicles crested a hill and went down the other side. At the bottom, the Civic turned into a small industrial park. Halfway down, it slowed, then came to a halt at the side of the road. A man jumped out the front passenger door and signaled to Kohler to pull into the driveway of the nearest warehouse on his right.

Kohler tugged the wheel and drove up the short driveway. Ahead, a steel door slid across on its rollers. He drove inside the building, pulled up to a stop, and killed the engine. Behind him, the gate rolled closed again and a set of fluorescent ceiling lights came on.

From his side window, he spotted a man emerge from the shadows and approach him. Kohler opened his window.

"*Don Max*, follow me," the man said.

Kohler got out and followed him over to where a prefabricated office had been installed on one side of the factory. Through the Perspex window, he saw Juancho sitting at a desk, surrounded by three men he'd never seen before. He walked up the steps and into the office.

"Good evening, Max. I trust you are well," the drug lord greeted him, rising to his feet. He spotted the day pack and pointed to one of his men. "Please, give the money to Rico."

Kohler shrugged off the pack and handed it to the man, who opened it up on the desk and began counting the money.

Kohler looked around the office. "The product?" he asked. "Where is it?"

Juancho placed a hand on his shoulder and ushered him back out of the office. By the side wall, a pallet lay on the floor, covered by a filthy tarp. Juancho leaned over and flung the cover back. Underneath, stacked neatly in rows several layers high, were dozens of brick-like objects, each one tightly wrapped in brown masking tape.

Kohler stared down at them and did a quick mental count. Each layer had five rows of nine bricks. There were four full rows while the fifth consisted of twenty more bricks. Two hundred in total.

"You wish to test it?" Juancho asked.

Kohler hesitated. This entire exchange was based on his trust of the drug lord. If he was being ripped off and confronted Juancho about it, he was in no doubt his life would end there and then. He shook his head. "It's okay. I trust you."

"I insist," Juancho said firmly. "Before the product leaves my hands, I need you to verify it. I cannot be responsible for its quality further down the chain. I have a reputation to maintain." He tipped his toe against the stack. "Go on. Choose one and test it."

"Very well." Kohler leaned over and selected a brick from the center of the pile. He placed it at the edge of the pallet and squatted beside it. From his pocket, he took out his Leatherman, selected the serrated blade, and sliced open the packet.

The powder was highly compressed. It took a ten-ton hydraulic press to make a kilo brick of cocaine. Kohler stuck the point of his knife deep inside it. Sometimes only a thin layer of the drug was stuck around a kilo of flour. Pride had got the better of him. He wanted to show the Colombian he knew what he was doing.

He took out one of several tester tubes he'd brought with him, and tipped approximately ten milligrams into it from the tip of the blade, then closed the lid and shook it hard for a few seconds.

With Juancho at his shoulder, he raised it up to the light. Both watched as the color of the liquid turned from green to dark brown. Kohler reached into his pocket again and produced a small color chart, placing it next to the vial. The color matched the darkest color at the bottom of the chart.

Juancho let out a satisfied grunt. "What a beautiful sight. It's almost off the chart."

Kohler nodded. "Eight-five percent pure or higher," he said.

Juancho smiled. "That's as good as it gets."

Kohler walked back over to the Toyota, popped the trunk open, and brought over several of the ammunition cases he'd brought with him. Then he, along with a few of Juancho's men, spent the next hour wrapping each brick in sheets of fabric softener and cling film. Stacking them upright, they fit five bricks into each of the .50 cal metal cases, snapping them closed once they were full.

When they had finished, Juancho ordered his men to load the forty ammo cans into the Toyota's trunk. Once the last one had been placed inside, Kohler did a quick count, then one of the men grabbed the tarp and spread it over the pile.

Kohler closed the trunk and locked it. Juancho, who had been watching the proceedings from nearby, came over. "All done? Excellent. See? We have both been true to our word. It gives me confidence that this will be the start of a wonderful friendship."

"I'm sure it will be." Kohler paused briefly. "Perhaps you might give me a means of contacting you directly so that I can let you know how everything went."

Juancho stared at him a moment, then took out a small notepad from his pocket and scribbled something on it. He tore off the page and handed it to Kohler. "You may email me at this address. Do it only via a secure VPN."

"Of course," Kohler replied, taking the note from him.

The drug lord stuck out his hand. "I wish you a safe journey, Max."

The two shook hands, then Kohler climbed into the Toyota, closed the door, and started the engine. Juancho barked out an order and, behind Kohler, the steel door slid back on its rollers.

He reversed out of the building where, on the street, the Honda Civic was waiting for him. It turned on its lights and headed back toward the entrance of the industrial estate. Moments later, Kohler was once more weaving through the back streets of Bogota as the Civic escorted him all the way back to the Avenida de las Americas. At the next lights, with a short blip of its hazard lights, it turned down a side street, leaving him alone on the busy highway.

Kohler blew out his cheeks, pleased with how the deal had gone down. Juancho had indeed been true to his word, and had delivered a high quality product. Even better, Kohler now had the means of contacting the drug lord directly, something he intended taking advantage of in the weeks to come.

He wasn't in a position to relax just yet, though, and kept a sharp eye on the street signs. When he reached Avenida Boyaca, he exited onto it via an overpass, and headed west. Fifteen minutes later, he was on the Autopista Sur, heading south out of the city and in the direction of Melgar.

Keeping to the center lane, and maintaining a steady speed of ninety kilometers an hour, his ETA back to the base was just over two hours. The rain had stopped, and he switched off his wipers. All the time, his senses remained on full alert, and he checked his mirror constantly to see if he was being followed. He didn't detect anything suspicious.

The next couple of hours passed uneventfully. Finally, ahead, a road sign loomed into view: *8km MELGAR*. He powered up his phone and punched in a memorized number.

After a couple of rings, a man's voice answered in Spanish. "*Si, digame.*"

"*Santiago…soy Max,*" Kohler said in halting Spanish. "*Estas por la puerta del base?*"

"*Si, teniente. Todo va bien. Estamos listo para ti.*"

"*Bueno, nos vemos in quince minutos,*" Kohler replied then hung up.

Tolemeida Airbase was located on the western outskirts of Melgar. The highway took him along the edge of the town where, at a large roundabout, he exited right. Moments later, he approached the entrance, a white arch with a huge pair of golden wings perched on top of it. A set of concrete bollards narrowed his approach, and brought him up to the main booth, where a security gate blocked his way.

Kohler stopped in front of it. Staring out the bulletproof window of the booth was Santiago. Behind him, his fellow guard, Carlos, sat reading a magazine.

Santiago stepped out of the booth and walked across to the Toyota, where Kohler proffered his ID though the window. After a quick inspection, Santiago returned it and saluted him. Kohler saluted back, then buzzed up his window. As he drove on, in his rearview mirror, he watched Santiago saunter back into the guardhouse. He breathed a sigh of relief. He'd made it safely back to the base.

He drove around to the main parking lot, where he slotted the Toyota in a space between two other vehicles. At 5 a.m. the next morning, he and the aircraft maintenance technician would drive over in a jeep, fetch the ammo cans, and load them onto the Hercules scheduled to fly out at 0800 hours that day.

He switched off his lights and killed the engine. From the corner of his eye, he spotted the headlights of a vehicle appear from around the side of a nearby building. A moment later, a second one appeared. Both were Jeeps. Kohler watched in horror as they raced across the tarmac and screeched to a halt on either side of him.

The doors opened, and several uniformed men spilled out of each. Pistols in hands, they surrounded the Toyota.

"Get out of the vehicle and raise your hands in the air!" one of them shouted in an unmistakable American accent.

His head spinning, Kohler reached for the door handle and got out. Slowly, he raised both arms.

"Step away from the vehicle."

Kohler did as he was told as two regular US soldiers strode over to him, both with pistols pointed at his chest. A third reached inside the Toyota and pulled out the ignition key. He went around to the back of the car and popped open the trunk. A moment later, there was the sound of one of the ammo cans being opened.

Several seconds passed, then the soldier closed the trunk and walked over to Kohler. On his shoulder sleeve, Kohler spotted an insignia only too familiar to him, that of a military police officer.

The MP stopped a few feet in front of him and looked him up and down. "Lieutenant Maxwell Kohler?" he asked in a clipped tone.

Kohler nodded, his throat to dry to speak.

"I am Captain Renfield, 11th MP Battalion, Fort Hood. I am investigating the alleged offense of drug trafficking in a Schedule 1 drug of which you are suspected. I advise you that under Article 31, UCJM, you have the right to remain silent, that is, say nothing at all. Any statement you make, oral or written, may be used as evidence against you in a trial by court martial, or in any other judicial or administrative proceedings."

As the MP continued to read him his rights, the military equivalent of a civilian's Miranda Rights, Kohler's mind raced. Who had betrayed him? Juancho or Mackenzie?

If it had been Juancho, why had he allowed two hundred kilos of pure cocaine to leave his hands? If it was Mackenzie, why would he forfeit a hundred and fifty thousand dollars for no more work than a few phone calls? Perhaps it was somebody else entirely.

As the captain escorted Kohler over to the waiting Jeep, he knew it didn't matter. Barring a miracle, he would spend the next decade of his life behind bars. Max Kohler was not a superstitious man. He didn't believe in miracles.

EXCERPT FROM THE MILITIA
THE NO DIRECTION HOME SERIES
BOOK FIVE

Tiffany awoke to a sudden gust of wind blowing through the trees. It stopped almost as soon as it had started. Raising her head, she saw that one of the tent flaps had blown open, and sunlight filtered into the room. Looking around, there was no sign of Chris.

With a sleepy yawn, she stretched her arms, and then checked her watch. It was 9:45 a.m., the latest she'd slept in since the pandemic first broke out. She and Chris had stayed up until dawn, making love until every square inch of her body ached. Even then, she hadn't stopped. Chris's desire had been insatiable, and though brutish at times, without a doubt it was the most fulfilling sex she had ever had. In all the years she'd been with Paul, she'd never experienced lovemaking that intense.

She ran a hand over her scalp. Its texture felt like sandpaper. It still shocked her to think how she looked as crazy as Chris now, though it gave her a certain thrill. Despite his strangeness, Tiffany realized that she had been attracted to him from the very first moment he'd strode out of the forest, crossbow in hand. Not that she'd had any idea then how things would turn out. She shook her head in wonder. The old world truly was dead and gone.

It was time to get on with the new. Gathering her clothes, she got dressed and headed over to the kitchen area. On the way, she glanced across to where Higgs and Cornel had set up their tents, and spotted Jade's pale blue one pitched next to theirs. Separate from the group, about twenty feet away, was a fourth tent, a brown one.

Poor Mark, all by yourself? Never mind, you'll have company soon enough.

There was no sign of anybody at the camp. She presumed Chris and Mark must be out hunting. Though Jade's tent was zipped up, Higgs and Cornel's were open. Inside, she could see both their backpacks. She smiled. As she suspected, Higgs hadn't gone anywhere.

In the hut that served as the larder, she found a large bag of oats, and another of sultanas. She tipped a little of both into a small steel pot, added water, and cooked it up. When it was ready, she poured condensed milk over the top, which she found in an already-opened can. Rummaging around the cutlery, she selected a clean spoon, and began eating her porridge straight from the pot.

I really am becoming a savage, aren't I? she thought to herself whimsically.

At the far side of the clearing, the one that led down to the river, she spotted Higgs and Cornel approaching. Bare-chested, wearing only sandals and shorts, both carried rolled-up towels under their arms and their hair was damp.

"How was your swim?" she asked when they reached her.

"Refreshing," Cornel replied, coming to a halt in front of her. His wiry frame looked tough and muscular, unlike Higgs who, though far bigger, was pudgy and out of shape.

Tiffany looked him up and down. "You need to lean out, Karl. If you put on some muscle, maybe you'll act tougher too. You know, when it really counts."

"Whatever." Higgs brushed past her and headed in the direction of his tent. "By the way, love the hair!" he called out over his shoulder. "Makes it easier to spot the crazy ones around here."

Chris and Mark were definitely out hunting. He wouldn't have dared say that so loudly otherwise. Ignoring Higgs's remark, Tiffany said, "That was fun last night, wasn't it, Cornel?"

A hint of a smile appeared on Cornel's lips. "Fun, no. Interesting, yes. We all learned something new about you." He draped his towel over the branch of a nearby tree. "I could do with a coffee. How about you?"

Tiffany shrugged. "Sure."

Cornel grabbed a pot and filled it from the water drum. Placing it on the stove, he lit the ring, then reached into the larder and pulled out two mugs, a jar of instant coffee, and a bag of sugar.

Tiffany waited until he'd dolloped a spoonful of coffee into each mug before speaking. "You know, as soon as Jade has recovered, Karl plans on getting out of here. He's not brave enough to leave on his own." She studied him a moment, her eyes flicking from one side of his face to the other. "How about you? You plan on leaving with them too?"

Cornel shook his head, though his eyes gave nothing away. "That would be stupid. Where would we go? I told you, I'm not going anywhere."

Tiffany smiled. "You're the smart one here, Cornel. That's become very clear to me."

"You're smart too, Tiffany. You just got off on the wrong foot. You're making up for it now, though."

The water had come to the boil. Cornel turned off the gas and poured it into the two mugs that he'd placed next to the stove. "Sugar?" he asked.

"One, please."

Cornel measured out a spoon, and began stirring. Tiffany stared at him. "I have a proposal for you. One that involves a big decision. Seeing how smart you are, I already know your answer."

Cornel stopped stirring and passed the mug over to her. "All right," he said softly. "What's on your mind?"

***

The rest of the morning passed uneventfully. After she finished talking with Cornel, Tiffany went back to bed and drowsed on and off for the next couple of hours. Slowly, her aching body started to feel normal again, other than the ache of wanting more.

Around 1 p.m., Chris and Mark returned with a slain buck, which Chris had shot with his crossbow. The two carried it into camp trussed upside down on a long pole. They took it down to the river, where they skinned and deboned it, then washed the meat to cool it. After wiping it dry, they cut it into thin slices and began smoking it in a tarp-covered tepee close to the kitchen.

"What about bears?" Tiffany asked anxiously, who'd come out to greet Chris when he'd first arrived back at the camp.

He shrugged. "We got to store it somewhere. Any bear that roams into this camp is going to leave with a dozen bullets in its hide."

After cleaning up, Chris entered the tent, where Tiffany was waiting for him. He flipped down the door flap and came over to sit beside her at the edge of the bed. Immediately, he reached across and began unbuttoning her short-sleeved hiking shirt.

Tiffany gently took away his hand. "Tonight," she said. "When I've fully recovered."

Chris grunted and lay down beside her. She waited a moment, until he was comfortable, before speaking. "You know, I was talking to Cornel earlier. We both remarked how well Jade is doing. She'll be back up on her feet in no time at all."

"Jade is strong," Chris replied. "I knew she would recover fast."

"Me too." Tiffany drew herself in closer to him. "Chris, there's something I've got to tell you..."

"What's that?"

"Cornel has come up with a great idea. Something that will help gel the tribe together." Tiffany reached a hand out and stroked his chest. "I'm sure you're going to think it's a great idea too."

FROM THE AUTHOR

For sneak peaks, updates on new releases and bonus content, subscribe to my mailing list at www.mikesheridanbooks.com.

THE MILITIA, Book 5 in the NO DIRECTION HOME series is out April 2018.

Printed in Poland
by Amazon Fulfillment
Poland Sp. z o.o., Wrocław